D0917666

BEACHFRONT CHRISTMAS

SOLOMONS ISLAND BOOK FOUR

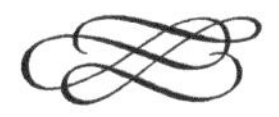

MICHELE GILCREST

CHAPTER 1

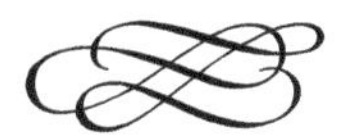

"Well, aren't you a sight for sore eyes?" Logan Woods said, standing six feet tall, well-dressed, and handsome. Logan was the owner of Virginia's largest boating company and requested a meeting to propose a business pitch to Lighthouse Tours. He extended his hands, introducing himself to Clara.

"Nice to meet you, Mr. Woods. I'm Clara Covington, Mike's office manager," she replied.

"Please, call me Logan. I recognize your beautiful voice from talking over the phone. I should start by thanking you for setting this up on such short notice. Most are still at home recovering from Thanksgiving dinner," he said, glancing at her ring finger.

Clara was happily engaged to Mike, the owner of Lighthouse Tours, and didn't mind twirling her ring so that Mr. Woods wouldn't get the wrong impression.

"It's not a problem. We try to keep the doors open as much as possible. This season we've been focusing a lot of our attention on rentals. You'd be surprised by how many locals like to get out on the water despite the cooler temps," she replied.

"Ha, right. I can imagine." Logan continued inspecting the surroundings, almost to the degree of being a little awkward.

"Why don't we make ourselves comfortable in the conference room," she said, leading him to the back. "Mike sends his apologies for not being able to join us. There was an issue with a leak at the North Beach office this morning. I assured him I would relay the details of today's meeting, but since I handle all things marketing related, I can assure you, you are in good hands."

"Yes, certainly. Please send my regards and let him know I look forward to having a face to face in the near future. If you don't mind me asking, how many employees do you have on staff at this location? It seems awfully quiet around here," he said, looking around.

They made themselves comfortable at the table where Clara could see blinking lights in her peripheral vision. The Christmas tree in the conference room was one of three that she worked tirelessly setting up to help spruce up the office.

"I always open up first thing in the morning. Ms. Mae, Jonathan, and Tommy should arrive in just a little while. Mr. Woods, I appreciate your sense of curiosity, but I think you expressed an interest in sharing a business idea which I'm dying to hear more about." She smiled.

"Yes." He reached into his briefcase and pulled out a packet, which he laid before Clara. On the front was an architectural layout of what appeared to be Lighthouse Tours, except the sign on the front said Solomons Shores.

"Before I get into the details, I should be upfront and share that I'm not here for marketing purposes. Instead, I have an interest in purchasing the business. I've been in the boating industry for a long time, covering everything from chartering private parties to rentals, tours, you name it. I even own several marinas. Basically, my track record speaks for itself," he said, handing her a business card and information about himself.

Clara shifted in her seat.

"I don't understand. Lighthouse Tours isn't for sale," she replied.

"Perhaps not at this very moment. I think by the time Mike reviews the numbers that I'm proposing, he'll be inclined to strongly consider his options. My proposal lays out the current value compared to what I'm willing to offer, which, believe me, is far above fair market value. I've also included expansion ideas that range from architectural enhancements, a complete overhaul of the dock, and the purchase of a nearby storage facility to house boats throughout the season. You see, I recently conducted a survey including locals in the area. It seems there's a dire need for a storage facility for the island, and that's something I'm able to invest in and have up and running by this spring."

She flipped through the first couple of pages of the packet then leaned back in her chair.

"Logan, while I would never speak for Mike, I'm almost certain he won't have an interest, no matter how attractive your offer may be. Lighthouse Tours is his baby... his heart and soul. He just ended a partnership of several years and was so excited to become the sole owner. It may not be as fancy as some of the ideas you've proposed, but—"

"May I call you Clara?" he interrupted.

"Sure."

"Good. Clara, I know it's a lot to take in. Which is part of the reason why I'd like to set up a meeting with Mike, directly. However, imagine what this could do for Solomons. The amount of increased revenue it would bring. And, more importantly, look at the amount of capital it would give Mike to further invest in his North Beach location," he said, pointing to the jaw dropping figure typewritten in bold and italics.

She studied the numbers for a brief moment and then looked up.

"But... if you took over Solomons, you would become our competition. That wouldn't make sense," she said.

"I wouldn't look at it that way. We'd practically be neighbors. Who knows, maybe we could even collaborate somehow. Trust me, it would be a win-win situation for everyone involved."

"Mr. Woods, I'm not so sure our employees would agree. Some have been with the company for well over a decade."

Logan scooted back from the edge of his seat with a smirk, seemingly admiring Clara while still trying to push his agenda.

He continued. "Mike mentioned you like to spearhead a lot of the marketing ideas for the company. He says you have a knack for drumming up new business. With your skill set, I'm sure you can recognize an excellent opportunity when you see one. Either way, here's what I'd like you to do. Take this package back to Mike. Tell him about my experience in the industry... maybe even look me up online if you're looking for more credibility. Most important of all, highlight these numbers," he said, pointing toward the financial column again. "Tell him I'll give him time to think it over, and then I'll give him a ring. This way we can talk business, man to man."

She clenched her teeth, trying very hard not to

react to his comment.

"By the way. That's a nice rock on your finger. Whoever managed to snatch you off the market is one lucky guy," he said, winking at her.

"Thank you. I'll have to share your sentiments with Mike. He's my fiancé."

Clara responded in the most upbeat voice she could muster up with a slight air of sarcasm, knowing he'd probably regret his coy approach.

"Pardon me. I did not know. Congratulations," he said.

"Thank you. I'll be certain to relay everything from our meeting and pass along the offer. If I don't see you beforehand, have a Merry Christmas, Mr. Woods."

He gathered his briefcase and rose from the table, extending his hand again.

"You can count on us seeing each other again. If Mike doesn't accept, I already have my sights set on the warehouse about a mile up the road and another property. One way or another Solomons Shores is making a new home for itself, right here on the island. If Mike is smart, he'll join forces and accept the offer of a lifetime. If not... well." He waited quietly and then added, "Let's just hope he's intrigued by my proposal."

Logan Woods nodded his head and wished Clara a good day, leaving her speechless at the conference table.

CHAPTER 2

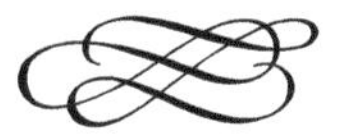

At the café, Mack popped a coin into their newly added and gently used juke box. It was a donation given by the bridge club that arrived just in time for Christmas. A holiday selection from the fifties played in the background as she joined Clara in a booth wearing a red Santa hat.

"I'm so excited about Christmas. I feel like a little kid in a candy shop. The café is decorated, business is booming now that folks are coming in from the cold, and... I actually have a special guy in my life for the holidays. I haven't been able to say that in ages." She lowered her voice while talking to her best friend.

"I'm so happy for you, Mack. Are you and Stephanie making plans with Brody this Christmas? I'll bet she would love to get him involved with decorating and exchanging gifts together," Clara replied.

"Stephanie is way ahead of you. She invited Brody to come with us to pick out the perfect tree and trim it all in the same day. You know how ambitious my little girl is. She has creatively thought of several plans for the upcoming weekends leading up to Christmas. The poor guy can't catch a break if he tried." She chuckled.

"I'm sure Brody is just as happy as he can be. I've always taken him as more of a family man."

"He really is, Clara. He invited us to meet his dad just before Thanksgiving. What a nice guy. Now I see where Brody gets his charm and respectful mannerisms from."

"That's wonderful. You deserve it." Clara smiled.

"Thanks, love. Hey, listen. Are you and Mike making plans for Christmas Eve? I've been working on a little surprise, and I'd really like for you two to be involved if at all possible."

"Mike's parents will be in town that week, but we'll be here. What did you have in mind?" Clara asked.

"Um, well, it's a secret. Sorry. I can't divulge the details, but let's just say... I have quite a few gift ideas to check off my Christmas list, and one in particular involves you and Mike. If you could carve an hour out of the evening to join us, that would be nice."

"I'm certain we can work something out, but it sure would be nice if you gave me a hint. Last year, you nearly gave the island a heart attack when you showed up at Christmas Nights dressed up as an elf. I know you did it for the kids, but I don't think we can handle any more surprises that involve you showing up with a pointy nose and pointy shoes." Clara laughed.

"Hey, I'll do anything once, and I'll always answer the call of duty for charity. Speaking of Christmas Nights, I haven't heard a peep about it this year. Have you?"

"No, which is kind of shocking since it's Solomons' annual Christmas tradition," Clara responded.

"I know. Normally by now we would see a crew decorating the storefronts, the island gazebo, and every business you can think of from here to the tip of the island. Then there's the tree lighting ceremony at the gazebo. How can we have a ceremony if we don't have a tree? I hope they don't drop the ball this year. It would be such a disappointment to the locals and the tourists."

"I'm sure they won't. Solomons Island has done a fantastic job of carrying out the tradition for as long as I've been living here. I'm sure they won't stop now. In the meantime, the only thing I can seem to think about is a meeting I had earlier this morning with a guy by the name of Logan Woods," Clara said.

"The name doesn't ring a bell."

Clara flipped through her cell phone and handed

it over to Mack. The screen revealed his picture on a website, along with his company information.

"Logan T. Woods, CEO, Virginia Boating Company. Hmm, I'm not sure that I follow. What's the big deal about Logan Woods?" Mack asked.

"Oh, no big deal. He just wants to buy out Lighthouse Tours and turn it into another one of his multi-million-dollar business ventures. I think he already has a name picked out. What did he call it again? Solomons Shores... yes, that's it."

"No! You're kidding me, right?" Mack asked.

"I wish I was."

"What did Mike have to say about this?" she asked.

"He doesn't know yet. He's been tied up all morning with a leak over in North Beach. I'll bet you a cup of coffee he will not be pleased. What really gets under my skin, besides the fact that Mr. Woods is a male chauvinist, is he already has plans for purchasing the warehouse about a mile up the road. That place is perfect for boat storage. He even said he's already surveyed the locals and believes that having a storage facility is a high priority."

"He could be stretching the truth or trying to scare you. I don't ever recall receiving a survey. I would remember something like that."

"Who knows what he's been up to. My radar tells me he's a snake, but whether or not I like the guy, just by searching online, he looks like he's doing very well for himself. Don't repeat this to anyone, but you should see the figures he's offering Mike to buy out Lighthouse Tours." Clara lowered her voice.

"It doesn't matter what he's offering. Lighthouse Tours is not for sale. Mike's been here for a long time. He's not going anywhere," Mack said.

"That's what I tried to tell him. But, this guy has the money to set up shop on the island whether Mike does business with him or not. I don't have a good feeling about this at all, Mack. Plus, his timing couldn't be worse... not that there's ever a good time for someone to show up and try to close down your shop... but still. Mike's parents are flying in for Christmas. It will be our first-time meeting. I just want him to be happy. No stress. No drama," Clara said, as she finished the last bite of her lunch.

"Everything will be fine. Mike will take care of it. Just wait and see. If you think for one minute the people of Solomons Island would let some loser with fat pockets come in here and put Lighthouse Tours out of business, think again. If I were you, I wouldn't lose an ounce of sleep over it."

Just then, Dakota, a new part-time server, greeted Mackenzie at the table.

"Hi, ladies. Can I get you a refill on your drinks?"

"Dakota, you'll have to forgive me. I almost forgot to introduce you to my best friend, Clara."

"Hi, nice to meet you," she said.

"Likewise," Clara responded, shaking her hand.

"Dakota will fill in for Josh when he's not here. You know he's been heavy into his auto parts business on the side. He says things have been picking up lately," Mack said.

"Wow, that's great. He's always had a knack for all things related to cars," Clara responded.

She then turned to Dakota.

"Are you from Solomons Island?" she asked.

"Technically, I was born here, but then my parents packed me up and moved all over the globe. I've lived everywhere from Germany to Hawaii, Texas, California... the list is endless."

"Marines...Navy?" Clara asked.

"Army brat." She giggled.

"Nice. What brought you back to Solomons?"

"Family. My grandmother lives here. You may know her. I believe everyone refers to her as Ms. Violet. She's a part of the bridge club," Dakota said.

"Ahh, you're Ms. Violet's granddaughter. Say no more. Everyone is going to love you around here. Welcome back to Solomons. If your kin folk to Ms. Violet, that means you have a built-in family here at the café."

"It already feels like it and I've only been here for a week," she said.

Mack chuckled. "And within that time, she's already doing a fantastic job. A customer already requested her by name. Josh better watch out. He has some tough competition on his hands."

"Thank you, ladies. Would you like me to give you a refill before I check on the other tables?"

"Sure, fill her up," Mack replied.

Once Dakota left, Clara and Mackenzie resumed their lunch break together.

"Okay, so I just thought of this, but I may have a plan for dealing with the guy who wants to buy Lighthouse Tours."

"I'm all ears," Clara responded.

Mackenzie checked her surroundings and then leaned in. "You could always shred the offer. When Mike asks you about the meeting, just downplay it like it was no big deal. After all... it's not a big deal because nobody's interested in the first place," Mack said.

"As much as I'd like to, I can't do that. Decisions about the business are solely up to Mike, and I'm not about to get our marriage off to a rocky start over it. Sorry, no can do."

Mack nodded in agreement. "I hear ya. I'm just trying to look out for all parties involved, that's all. Speaking of getting married... have you set a date yet?"

"Honestly, we haven't. We tossed around the idea of getting married next summer, but I kind of like the idea of waiting until our busy season simmers down. Mike is flexible either way. Right now, I'm really focused on meeting his folks. We were all bummed about not seeing each other in September. I figure once I meet them and get the nervous jitters out of my system, then I can concentrate on wedding plans," she said.

"Aww, I'm sure you have nothing to be nervous about. They're going to love you, Clara."

"I hope so."

"Girl, what's not to love?" Mack asked.

"What about you and Brody? It sounds like he's getting along great with Stephanie, but how's the relationship going?"

"Let's just put it this way. Having Brody in my life makes me wonder what I ever saw in the men I knew before him. He's gentle and kind. He actually listens to me when I speak. And he pays attention to the little details, Clara. You don't understand. I never knew this kind of man existed. Sometimes I have to pinch myself to make sure I'm not dreaming," she replied.

"That's funny, but I can assure you Brody is the real deal. We have a lot of nice guys who work for us between Solomons and North Beach, but Brody has a heart of gold. If you repeat that to the others I'll deny it all day, but between us, it's true."

"Well, that's very reassuring coming from you. Hey, how's your sister doing these days? Last time I saw her, she was all fired up about potentially starting her food truck in the spring. How's that going?" Mack asked.

"I don't know how she does it. She literally works

multiple shifts at the Seafood Shack, and then gets off work and spends the entire day making phone calls to one licensing agency or another. Ever since I offered to help invest in a truck, she's been on a mission to make it work. I have to admit, I wasn't sure how she would do with getting back on her feet and making a living for herself, but I'm proud of her. She's really making it work."

"Hey, some of us just need an extra push, that's all. She's going to flourish out here on the island. All she needed was a fresh start... and a rekindled relationship with you." Mack smiled.

"Agreed. Ooh, I have to run. It's late," Clara said, checking her watch.

She placed a shawl around her shoulders, wrapping herself up and grabbing her purse.

"Please tell chef Harold we are patiently awaiting his homemade hot chocolate. I know he likes to crank out his first batch every year on December first, but we really need to talk him into moving the tradition up a bit, don't you think?" Clara asked.

"Ha, good luck with that one. I'll work on him, but he knows exactly how he likes to run his kitchen." Mack laughed.

"All right. I'll see you later."

"Later, girlie. Keep me posted about the other situation. Let me know if there's any way the staff here at the café can help," Mack said and winked as she walked away.

CHAPTER 3

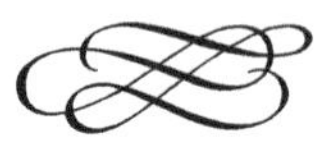

Mike pulled into Clara's driveway just as the sun set with takeout for two. With Thanksgiving behind them and all the leftovers gone, it was the least he could do to bring her something... and a good excuse to see his bride to be. Not that he needed one.

"Mmm, let me guess, today you're wearing sweet vanilla mist?" he said, while entering the house, stopping briefly to nestle his nose against her cheek.

"Yep. My mom used to always say a lady should never leave the house without wearing her signature scent. I'm starting to think you've memorized the name of every bottle I own by name." She teased.

"Only because it smells so good on you," he replied, smiling at her.

Mike headed to the kitchen, unpacking an array

of selections from the local Chinese restaurant, and spread everything on the counter.

"I sure hope you're hungry. I ordered enough food to feed an army. We have General Taos Chicken, Lo mein, pork fried rice, regular rice, steamed dumplings..." He continued.

She raised her hand to her hip and stared at him. "I'm convinced you have a tapeworm in your body, Mike Sanders. We can't eat all this food."

"Hey, speak for yourself. I'm starving. What should've been a one or two-hour job with the plumber turned into an all-day event. Our secretary, Jan, is going to be so upset when she sees all the water damage that was done to her ornaments and Christmas decorations."

"That's terrible. Were you able to at least salvage the carpet and furniture in the front lobby?" she asked.

"Yeah, it will be fine. He's using a big industrial fan to dry everything out. Leaks are to be expected every now and again. It's an older building and we all know that old buildings come with occasional issues. We will not let a minor pipe leak impede the holiday spirit. Not if I have anything to do with it."

"Good. I like the way you think. Now let's see if you can manage to keep the same positive attitude once I tell you about my meeting with Logan today," Clara said, pecking him on the nose.

"That doesn't sound good," he responded.

Just then, Clara's sister Agnes walked in.

"I thought I caught a whiff of Chinese food on the way coming in. Wow, what a spread. Do you have extra? I'll pay you for it," she offered, poking around the trays of food to see what options were available.

"Sure. It's not like we were having a private date night or anything. Help yourself." Clara teased.

"Oops. Sorry. I can always come back later to check for leftovers. I worked a double shift today and barely had time to eat."

Mike and Clara looked at each other, releasing a little laughter.

"So much for my tape worm," he said.

"What was that?" Agnes asked.

"Nothing. Grab a plate and help yourself. Free of charge. Seriously, there's plenty to go around," Mike offered.

"Are you sure? I don't want to intrude."

"We were teasing, Agnes. Go ahead and grab yourself a plate. While you're at it, I'd love to hear how things are going at the new job. All you ever do is come in late and creep downstairs to the basement. I take it things are going well?" Clara asked.

"It couldn't be better. The people are nice and the tips are great. Every bit counts these days. I've been stashing away as much as I can to save up for the licensing and fees to get the food truck up and running in the spring," Agnes said.

"Do you really think you'll be able to pull it off that soon?" Mike asked.

"I don't see why not. When Clara offered help with buying the truck, that was half the battle. When I'm off, I work diligently filling out applications, planning my menu, and investigating every angle of this business, ensuring a successful launch. I'm determined to make it work, Mike. The diner is great, but there's nothing like making it on your own."

"Okay, just know if you need any help from a business standpoint, I'm here and happy to answer questions," he offered.

Agnes followed Clara and Mike around the counter, filling her plate with everything that would satisfy her appetite.

"Ooh, I almost forgot to mention that you and Mike have a message from the mayor's secretary on your answering machine. She apologized for bothering you at home but was hoping to arrange an appointment to meet as soon as possible," Agnes said.

Clara's eyebrows folded together. "Mayor Thompson's office?"

"Yep, that's the one. I meant to text you this morning, but I got distracted."

"Hmm. That's odd. Mike, do you have any business with Mayor Thompson?" Clara asked.

"Back in the summer, we met about putting on a potential parade or boat show for the fourth, but because of a time crunch, nothing ever came of it. That's the only thing I can think of," he responded.

"Well, I guess the only way to find out is to give them a ring first thing in the morning. Mae must've given them my number. I'll have to look into it," Clara said.

"Isn't that sweet? The two lovebirds have a personal connection with the town mayor. I swear you guys and the people of this island are like something straight out of a movie. So picture perfect." Agnes giggled, shaking her head.

"Oh, and uh... you might want to look above your heads. One of Santa's little helpers may have planted some mistletoe in random places around the house." Agnes grabbed her utensils and a soft drink and slowly backed out of the kitchen as Clara and Mike looked up, smiled, and then kissed.

Afterward, they settled in the dining room for a peaceful dinner for two.

"Where were we?" Mike asked.

"I think we were trying to figure out why Mayor Thompson's office is tracking us down."

"No, you were just about to tell me about your meeting with Logan Woods. I looked him up online. He's seems pretty reputable," Mike said.

"Oh, he's reputable all right. I looked him up as well. As a matter of fact, he encouraged me to do so. He owns more than one boating company in the state of Virginia and several marinas. The guy is loaded."

"Yeah, which makes me wonder why he would waste his time trying to do business with us," he said.

"Unfortunately, he doesn't want to do business with us as much as he wants to put us out of business." She excused herself from the table and grabbed the offer out of her bag in the foyer.

"He portrays himself as a businessman, but in my opinion, he's nothing short of a city slicker looking to get over. When he wasn't flirting, he asked questions about how many people we had on staff, and then slapped this bad boy down on the table."

She passed him the packet. Mike continued forking the next piece of chicken while reading it over.

"Solomons Shores?" he asked.

"Yep. That's what he plans to name Lighthouse Tours once he buys it out."

"Whoa. Wait one minute. Buy what out? The business is not for sale," he said.

"Which is exactly what I tried to tell him, but he seemed to think the offer would impress you just the same. Flip the page and check out how much he's willing to pay. He says it's above market value, not that I believe a word coming out of his mouth."

"Wow. Very interesting. Well, I'll give him an A for effort, but sorry. I'm not going for it. Lighthouse Tours just officially became mine and I'm not about to give it up, regardless of how much he offers. Just follow up with him and let him know I reviewed everything, but we're not interested," Mike said.

"I wish it were that easy." Clara laid her fork down.

"Mike... there's more. He said he surveyed the locals and from what he gathered, everyone has a need for a nearby facility that can shrink-wrap and store their boats for the winter." She continued.

"Yeah, okay, so we'll work on it. Right now, we're able to house a few boats. It might be minimal, but when we continue to grow and can set aside the capital for a down payment, we can expand. Maybe even look at the warehouse about a mile up the road at some point."

She placed her hand over his.

"He said if you're not interested, he plans to purchase the warehouse and have it up and running by the spring. One way or another, he's bringing his business idea to the island. I think this was just a courtesy meeting to give you an opportunity to get in on the action, or prepare for competition."

"Did he say that?" he asked.

"Well... not exactly, but he was pretty clear that Solomons Island is where he wants to be this upcoming spring. This guy is easily used to running a multi-million-dollar operation, Mike. What are we going to do?"

Mike slouched back in his chair, relinquishing his fork.

"I'm going to call him first thing in the morning and let him know I'm not interested. I don't take too kindly to threats, and frankly, I think it's poor business practice to take this kind of approach," he said.

"That's right, babe. Stand up for what is yours. Don't let him intimidate you."

Mike continued thinking the situation over.

"The only thing that baffles me is why the locals haven't mentioned anything about their storage needs to me. This makes me wonder if they're already seeking other means, and if eventually, I'll start to lose their business," he said.

"Mike, I don't know what would make you say that. Everyone loves you and your boat tours. Then there's the newly added boat rentals, which is doing very well. You can't do it all."

"Why not? Look, I'm not trying to dominate the industry out here by any means. But Solomons is a small island to begin with. If we call ourselves an expanding business that now focuses on not just tours, but rentals, and all things boat related, then we need to catch up with the times and have a proper storage facility. Right now people look to us, but if we don't get our act together, guys like Logan Woods can quickly put us little guys out of business."

Clara sighed.

"Perhaps I picked the wrong time to tell you about this. It's been a long day and maybe you need to unwind. You know, give your mind a break and tackle this tomorrow. The last thing I wanted to do is stress you out. You've barely finished your food. Come on, I can tell you're getting frustrated. Let's shake it off for now. Come over here and sit closer to me," she said.

Mike wore a doubtful expression on his face.

"I'll be fine," he said.

"Mike," Clara responded, slowly dragging out his name and refusing to give in.

"Really, I'm good. This isn't exactly something I want lingering in the back of my mind right before the holidays, but I'm good. I'll call him tomorrow and be done with it."

Clara walked to the head of the table, positioning herself behind him, and began kneading her hands into his shoulder blades. The tense muscles in his body relaxed, giving in to her touch.

"Have I told you how much I love you lately?" he asked.

"Hmm, I don't recall hearing it within the last hour."

"Ha, well, let me take care of that. Clara Covington, I love you and I love how supportive you are," he said.

Mike reached over his shoulder and slipped his hand over hers. "I know you want to take your time choosing a wedding date that's just right. One that will accommodate all of our family and friends. I just want you to know when that day comes, I'll be so proud to call you Mrs. Sanders."

"I sure hope so. We make a pretty good team, if I say so myself. Plus, I hate to break it to you, but it's a done deal now. The minute you planted this beauty on my finger, I knew there was no turning back." She teased.

CHAPTER 4

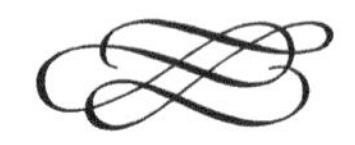

On Monday, Jonathan and Mae spent their evening sorting through bins filled with Christmas lights. Since they both worked at Lighthouse Tours, they spent most evenings and weekends catching up on preparations to host their family at the end of the month. This week's task included outdoor lighting, the least favorite on Jonathan's honey-do list.

"Mae, I can't figure out for the life of me why you have so many of these net lights. If you tested any of them, you'd realize that most only light up halfway."

"Yes, but if you combine two nets together, you can cover an entire bush, Jonathan. See, all you have to do is mesh them together and presto..."

Mae plugged in the two nets. Half of one lit up

with blue bulbs, the other lit halfway in the color green.

"Good grief. These are all mix matched and some of them have bulbs missing. There is such a thing called a replacement bulb, you know," he grumbled, shaking his head.

"That's why I have you, dear. I've never been good at the details. Just keep digging. There should be enough to go with an all green, blue, or white theme. As long as we make it festive for the grand-kids, that's all that matters to me," Mae said.

"Mmm hmm."

Mae continued. "I spoke to my sister Rose during lunch. She's excited about coming to visit in a couple of weeks. She offered to help with the cooking and said she'd be glad to share a room with the grands if we needed the extra space." She smiled.

"I haven't seen Rose in so long, it will be nice catching up with her."

"That makes two of us. You know how it is with us. We don't talk regularly, but when we get together, it's like we never miss a beat. Unfortunately, this year, she, among other family members, are still giving me a hard time about eloping. Hopefully, our time together for the holidays can help make up for it," Mae replied.

"Yep, they'll be fine once we all get together. What about Lily? Did she mention when her, Steven, and the kids plan on joining us for Christmas?"

"Let's see... Rose will be here around the twentieth, which means Lily and the gang won't arrive until a couple of days later. You know the kids don't get out of school until it's almost Christmas Eve."

"Are they staying until the New Year?" he asked.

"I sure hope so. What about your sister, Andy? Have you confirmed a date with her?"

"Sadly, it looks like Andelle won't be able to make it," he said, dragging the bins out to the front lawn.

"Why not?" Mae asked.

"Because she's been having more trouble than expected since her surgery. She thought it might be best to not travel and stay close to home and rest. I can't blame her. We'll have to get a care package together and send it to her."

"Certainly."

"Mae."

"Yes."

"If I'm going to successfully get through all this decorating tonight, I need a little motivation," he said.

"We're outside, love. How about we save the motivation for later on tonight... think of it as an incentive for getting the lights done."

Jonathan smiled, revealing a few creases on both sides of his eyes.

"While I'll never turn down an invitation to your sweet lovin, I was actually referring to a hot cup of coffee." He chuckled.

Just then Meredith, their next-door neighbor, stepped outside with a trash bag in hand. She was just in time to catch Jonathan in the middle of giving Mae a kiss.

"Oh, for crying out loud. Either I always have terrible timing, or you two never stop slobbering over one another," she said, making her way to the side of the house where she kept the trash bin.

Mae laughed loud enough for the neighbors to hear a couple of doors down.

"Good evening, Meredith. We're just out here fiddling with the lights, that's all. Your decorations look lovely. Did your son come by and help you?" Mae asked.

"No, he's busy with his new job. I hired a company this year. I thought it might be nice to have the lights up and running around the same time as the gazebo in the center of town, but it looks like I beat them to it this year. Apparently, somebody on the island is behind schedule this year," Meredith replied.

"Now that you mention it, I wonder what's going on. There hasn't been one flyer or announcement about Christmas Nights since the Thanksgiving holiday began," Jonathan said.

Meredith came closer to the fence between their properties and leaned over.

"I'm not sure, but I'll tell you one thing... as the HOA president of this community, I think it's high time we do something fun. In the spirit of Christmas, tomorrow morning you'll have a friendly invitation from myself and the board to join our neighborhood decorating contest. We understand everyone has busy schedules, therefore hired help is allowed."

"Oh, for Pete's sake," Jonathan mumbled in a low voice as he continued separating the lights.

"I'm sorry, what was that, Jonathan?" Meredith asked.

"Just clearing my throat. Carry on."

"The winning house in the community will receive Chef Harold's homemade hot chocolate free for the entire month of January, along with one free meal for the family, complements of the café." Meredith was beaming proudly at the idea.

"That explains all the illuminated candy canes lining your driveway," Mae replied.

Meredith glanced back at her house and then looked at their bucket of lights, mangled and twisted in every direction.

"Looks like you have an awful lot of work ahead of you. I'll leave you to it. If I run into Mayor Thompson, I'll see if I can get the inside scoop on what the island is planning to do this year for Christmas Nights. In the meantime, be on the lookout for the flier. I know competition is going to be fierce," she said, with a huge grin as she walked away, returning to her front door.

Jonathan and Mae looked at each other and then looked at their bucket. If ever there was a time to purge the old lights and splurge on a new set, now was the time.

~

"Logan... it's Mike Sanders. How are you?" he asked, putting on his most confident and professional voice on the other end of the telephone line.

"Mike, what a pleasant surprise. I didn't expect to hear from you so soon."

"Yes, my apologies for not being able to meet with you. I had my hands full with a leak at my other business location," Mike said.

"Clara shared the news. Sorry to hear it. I hope everything turned out okay," Logan replied.

"Everything is fine. These things happen every now and again. It comes along with the territory of owning property," he said, trying to sound polite.

"Yes, indeed. Well, I would imagine if you're calling it means you reviewed my proposal," Logan said.

"I did. I have to admit you caught me off guard for a moment there. It's not every day that someone drops by offering to purchase the shop, which is not for sale."

"Understood. I'll admit my business practices are unconventional, but it's part of the reason why I'm so successful at what I do. That plus, I invest a lot of time in doing my research, and I listen to the needs of the people… all of it making a good recipe for a thriving business." Logan paused, waiting for Mike to offer feedback.

"Interesting. Well, from the looks of things, you're operating a thriving business across the state line in Virginia. What's the fascination with Solomons Island?"

"Ha, I'm in it for the same reason you are. The money. I have the vision, the manpower, the marketing team, and the capital to turn Lighthouse Tours into a well-oiled money-making machine. I can double, if not triple the number of tours going out. Plus, I'll be able to provide more than adequate storage space for the locals by the spring, and to seal the deal, I can even build a full-service marina. Solomons Island won't know what hit them. I mean this in a good way, of course. They'll thank me for bringing more business to the island. More business means more food on the table. Isn't that what it's really all about?" he asked.

Mike drew in a deep breath, exhaling ever so quietly as not to reveal his growing frustration.

"To be honest… no. That's not what it's all about. Respectfully, your plan sounds amazing to someone who's only looking at the numbers, but anybody who knows the true heart of Solomons knows that big city ideas won't stand a chance on the island," Mike said.

"I beg to differ. After mailing out surveys to a good portion of the residents, you'd be surprised at just how many of them would be thrilled about having a larger facility to store their boats. A place that wouldn't require them to go off island is a reasonable request, don't you think?"

"Okay, so there's room for improvement... but I stand by my opinion... Solomons Island isn't looking for some big time Hollywood type operation to come along and flood the area. It's just not what we're about," Mike said.

"I take it by your response that you're not interested in my offer?"

Mike cleared his throat, looking once more at the figures outlined on page three. Then he closed the packet.

"While your offer is generous, I'm afraid I have to decline. I have something invested in this business that could never be replaced with money, and that's my love for the people and my blood, sweat, and tears. I won't trade that in to make a quick buck. Sorry, Mr. Woods, but as my fiancé stated earlier, the business is not for sale."

Logan let out an unsettling chuckle on the other end of the line.

"No problem. I understand you have your attachments to the place and all. By any chance, did your fiancé mention anything about my alternative plans?" he asked.

"Clara said something about the warehouse. Listen, Logan, no matter which way you slice it, I just wanted to offer the courtesy of calling you back. I'm pretty sure you have just as much of a full plate as I do with the holiday season."

"Right. Well, thank you for your time, then. It's highly likely that we'll be neighbors soon. I'll be seeing you around. Take care."

Logan hung up, leaving Mike listening to a silent telephone line, and contemplating just how far he was willing to go.

CHAPTER 5

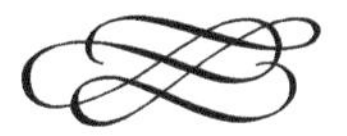

Mackenzie jumped, startled at the sight of broad hands quickly covering her eyes from behind. Brody's jovial voice put her at ease, causing her to smile and wonder what he was up to.

"Surprise," he said.

"Brody, you're lucky I like you. If anyone else walked up to me like that I'd have to swing first and ask questions later," Mack said, laughing wholeheartedly.

"Hey, I have to keep you on your toes," he said, reaching toward a rose he laid down on a nearby table.

"Aww, how sweet? I guess I'll forgive you this time... but only because of the romantic gesture." She smiled.

Brody and Mackenzie had been dating since the

summer. She knew him for much longer from Lighthouse Tours, but only recently opened up to the idea of a relationship. She loved that he was spontaneous and adoring... and more importantly she loved that he was taking his time building a relationship with her daughter, Stephanie. It was one of her top requirements if he wanted to enter the gateway to her heart.

"What brings you here with a rose in hand on a Monday afternoon?" she asked, twirling the flower between her fingers.

Brody looked around before answering.

"Have you looked in the mirror lately? If it was feasible, I'd stop by here every day of the week just to catch a glimpse of you," he said.

In the background, Josh walked by with a pitcher of coffee in hand and interrupted. "Okay, so let's cut to the chase here, people. You two adore one another — I'm talking head over heels, I get it. But, practically the whole café, including myself, wants to know when you plan on making this thing official? It doesn't take long to figure out if you want to be exclusive — heck, maybe even consider tying the knot for the holidays? I dunno. Give us something to work with here," Josh said, as he refilled a cup for a nearby customer.

Mack gave him a look.

"Josh, I could've sworn you had somewhere to be. I believe the young lady over at table three needs your assistance," she said.

"Mmm hmm. Okay, I know how to take a hint. But, this conversation isn't over. By the way, I need to take tomorrow morning off, please and thank you. Brody, it was good seeing you." Josh acknowledged Brody and leaned over to whisper, "Whatever you're doing, it's making her a very happy woman, so keep up the good work. If she's happy, then we're all happy."

"Thanks, man. I'll keep that in mind," Brody said, slapping him on the back as he laughed.

Mack wore a smirk on her face. "I'm telling you, the minute I started developing a love life, everyone around here has given the word inquisitive a whole new meaning." Mack complained.

"It's only because they care and they want to see you happy. I can't say that I blame them. You have nothing to worry about. The pressure is really on me," Brody said.

"How so?"

"Think about it... the whole island knows me by name, and I work right across the street. Josh is right, if I don't keep you happy, who do you think they'll come looking for?" he asked.

Mack swatted her dish towel at his chest. "Oh, Brody, stop. That's nonsense and you know it. Our relationship is no one's business but our own. No matter what he says." She emphasized.

"So... is it okay to call it that... an exclusive relationship?"

It had been a while since she made it past six weeks of dating. Their length of time together was by far a miracle, so she didn't quite know what to say. She fumbled for a moment.

"Uh, sure... I guess it's to be expected by now... right?"

"Only you can answer that question. Does it feel right to you? That's something only you would know on the inside. Right around this area — over here," he said, pointing to her heart.

Mack nervously checked to see who was watching and then locked eyes with Brody.

"Yes. Of course, I want to be exclusive with you. You've been so loving and kind to me and my baby girl. How could I refuse that kind of love?" she said, placing her arms around him tugging on his broad neck.

Brody squeezed Mackenzie, picking her off the floor before gently placing her back down.

"If we weren't standing in the middle of your workplace and didn't have an audience, I promise I'd plant a big one on you." He smiled, whispering into her ear.

"You are so bad — and I love every bit of it. How about we save that sweet moment for later on?" she asked.

"Sounds good. Oh, and before I forget. The real reason I stopped by is to ask you and Steph out on a date. I was thinking this Friday might be nice to build a bonfire on the beach and maybe roast a few smores. I'll bring a few blankets if needed."

"That sounds nice. I know Steph will be over the moon when I tell her," Mack replied.

"Great. I have to head back to the dock, but I'll call you tonight." Brody walked backward toward the door, nearly bumping into another customer. He waved with a huge smile on his face and then exited, making his way across the street.

"Good night of living. What on earth have you done to that man?" Josh teased, shaking his head at the sight of Brody fumbling on his way out the door.

"Is that jealousy I detect in your voice?" she asked.

"Who me? No, ma'am. I'm perfectly happy by myself. I have a job, a part-time business, and I dog sit for my neighbor whenever she's out of town. Does that sound like the life of someone who has time for a girlfriend?" he asked.

"It sounds like the life of someone who fills their time with a ton of things to keep from being lonely, but don't worry. I'll keep my eye out and have you fixed up with someone in no time. She could show up when you least expect it, so get your ducks in a row and be ready."

"No, thank you. I'll live vicariously through you and the Brodster," Josh replied.

"Oh, don't be a Scrooge."

"Mackenzie, if you even think about trying to set me up with someone, so help me..." he threatened.

"All right," she said, putting her hands up. "Do it your way. I've never met anyone who prefers being alone for the holidays, but have it your way."

Back at Lighthouse Tours, Mae, Jonathan, Mike, and Clara were gathered around the front desk talking when a messenger arrived with an envelope.

"Good afternoon, I have a delivery via Island Express for Mike Sanders. Is he here today?" the messenger asked.

"I'm Mike Sanders," he responded, stepping forward.

"Ah, Mr. Sanders, I just need your signature right here and this envelope is all yours."

The gentleman handed him an electronic device with a pen attached. Mike could barely make out his signature on the screen, but scribbled as best as he could and handed the device over.

"These machines make me miss the good old days back when we used a thing called pen and paper." Mike chuckled.

"I'm with you, sir. It seems like everything is electronic these days. Sometimes I think we're too advanced for our own good."

"Exactly," Mike responded.

He took the envelope and thanked him for his service. Afterward, he grabbed a letter opener, eagerly ripping through the envelope to dive into its contents.

"Thirty-day notice... Hmm, what is this?" he said, talking out loud to himself.

Clara and Mae inched closer to listen in.

"It says that Lighthouse Tours has approximately thirty days to remove all of its business equipment from the docking area associated with building number three twenty-one and three twenty-two. If we don't comply, we could be fined, and they could confiscate the equipment. This has to be some sort of mistake," he said.

"Who is the letter from?" Clara asked.

"The clerk's office. Building three twenty-one and twenty-two cover our place and the docking area of the store adjacent to us. The place next door is vacant and has been for a while now. Regardless, the entire docking area in the back of these buildings came with this property when Ken and I bought the building. This has to be some sort of mistake," he said.

"Don't worry, boss. I'm sure it can easily be fixed. There are a few new people taking over at the clerk's office. It's probably an error," Jonathan said.

As they stood around discussing the matter, Clara noticed someone from Solomons Reality parking outside of the store next door. The place was empty and had been for several months with a for sale sign in the front window. She watched as the realtor got out of the car.

"Well, I'm not sure what the notice is all about, but maybe that realtor knows something we don't. Maybe we should catch up to her and see if you can get some information," Clara said.

"Clara is right. It may be worth your time," Mae offered.

"I don't see how she can be helpful since this is about something I already own," he responded.

"Mike, it can't hurt. Just tell her you're curious to know if they found anyone who's interested in buying the store, then see if you can get her to talk about the dock in the back." Clara nudged.

"How about I get on the phone with the clerk's office and you go play detective on my behalf?" he asked, revealing a crease in between his eyebrows. It was always easy to tell when Mike was stressed. It's usually when he became laser focused and was terrible at utilizing his poker face.

"I'm on it." Clara disappeared next door and Mike made his way to his office. Once at his desk, he tapped a few buttons and had the clerk's office on speaker phone ready to demand an explanation. Within moments, someone picked up the phone.

"Clerk's office, how may I help you?" a woman answered.

"Hi, this is Mike Sanders, over at Lighthouse Tours. How are you?"

"I'm well, sir. How can I help you today?"

"I'm calling regarding a notice I received about removing my business equipment. I would assume they're referring to the rental equipment, and some items owned by a few of my customers," he said.

"Hold on. Let me transfer you to the right department."

Mike sat back in his chair, listening to Christmas music on the telephone line as he waited.

In the meantime, Jonathan came to the door and whispered, "Mae and I will be out back helping a customer with one of the sailboats."

Mike gave him the thumbs up.

"Hello."

"Hi, Mike Sanders here. I'm calling regarding a notice that was delivered."

"What's the reference number on your notice? It should be a six-digit number on the right-hand side of the sheet."

He called off the numbers one by one.

"Yes, I have you right here in the system. It looks as if you're in violation of utilizing property that doesn't belong to you."

"That can't be. I have the paperwork from when my former business partner and I bought the place. We've been in operation here for a long time now.

How is it that the other businesses share the same understanding about the dock, but you guys seem to be confused?" Mike asked, fidgeting with pen on his desk.

"Please don't shoot the messenger. If you think there's a discrepancy, the best thing to do is bring a copy of your deed down to the clerk's office and we can match your records with ours. By the way, did you say you have a co-owner in the business? I don't see anyone else in the system but you. It looks like you purchased the property by yourself within the past year, correct?" she asked.

"Yes, I was referring to Ken, the guy I originally bought this property with before I took it over. Either way, I have all my ducks in a row and can bring everything down to you this afternoon."

"Okay, we'll be here. Is there anything else I can help you with, Mr. Sanders?"

He looked up to the sight of Clara, who was slightly out of breath.

"No, I'm good. Thank you."

"Happy holidays," she bellowed.

"Same to you," he said, sounding melancholy as he hung up.

Clara jumped right in. "Are you ready for this?"

"Whatever it is, has to be better than the conversation I just had with the clerk's office."

"I'm not so sure. According to the realtor, someone called expressing a strong interest in the place next door this morning. She wouldn't reveal any names, but she confirmed that it's another boating company. They also inquired about the warehouse up the road, and one other location that's hitting the market around the first of the year."

"Next door? You're kidding me," Mike snapped.

"I wish. This has Woods' name written all over it. No one from Solomons Island would pull a stunt like this."

Mike got up and paced around, trying to pull his thoughts together.

"Did she give you any other details... particularly about the dock... or anything?" he asked.

"Nope. She just said he called to inquire but seemed very interested."

"Yeah, well, on my end, they're trying to claim that a portion of the dock doesn't belong to us. Horrible timing if you ask me," Mike grumbled.

"That sounds like the least of your worries. All you have to do is show them the proof. I'd be more concerned about Woods. Making room for him on Solomons Island is a recipe for disaster."

Mike walked over to his filing cabinet to rummage through several folders. One by one, he tossed certain files out of the way until he stumbled upon a folder with the word deed written at the top.

"Here it is," he said, confidently holding the file in the air. "I think I'm going to head over to the clerk's office now. We can look into this whole thing with Woods when I get back," he said.

"Mike, we have an appointment with Mayor Thompson in a couple of hours. His secretary said he has a tight schedule this afternoon."

"No problem. As soon as I'm done at the clerk's office, I'll swing back around and pick you up," he replied.

"Mike..."

"Yes?"

"Everything is going to be just fine. We'll tackle one hurdle at a time. Then, before you know it, your parents will be here, and we can get back to celebrating the Christmas season."

Clara placed both hands on his shoulders, reassuring him.

CHAPTER 6

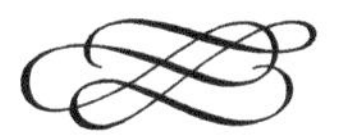

"Jonathan, what gave you the idea of sneaking away for a lunch date?" Mae asked.

"Ha, that's an easy one. I looked across the dock and thought to myself, when is the last time you did something spontaneous for that gorgeous woman of yours." He chuckled.

"You do something for me all the time, Jonathan."

"That's because a wise man once taught me you can never be too good to your woman."

"Was the wise man your father?" she asked.

"Yes, ma'am. He adored my mother... treated her like a queen. There was nothing in the world he wouldn't do for her... not a thing."

"Aww, that's sweet, darlin. I'll bet you and your brother learned more from his actions than words could ever express. To think I would be so lucky to reap the benefits of his example. I don't take it for granted."

Mae reached for her thermos filled with warm tea as they kicked back in his pickup truck. It had been a few months since they last visited the same spot on the beach where Jonathan proposed.

"How do you like our latest addition to the Christmas decorations?" he asked, pointing to the hood of the truck.

"I figured if we're going to be a part of this silly contest, we might as well go all out. Reindeer ears for the top of the truck and a red nose that lights up the hood ought to get Meredith's attention," he said.

"Oh, Jonathan, that's terrible. I love the reindeer look, but the whole point of joining the contest is getting into the spirit of the holidays and building a sense of community. It's not an actual competition."

"To me it is. I'm tired of Miss Busy Body always poking her nose around and stirring up trouble. Doesn't she have enough to do as a board member of the HOA? Good grief." He complained.

Mae chuckled.

"In your defense, we didn't hire a fancy company to do our decorations like she did, but we're giving the neighborhood a run for their money. More importantly, we're creating a fun place for the grandkids to come and visit. I can't wait to see the looks on their faces," she said.

"That makes two of us. In the meantime, you know what else I can't wait to see?"

"Jonathan, don't start. We're out here in the middle of broad daylight on the beach, for goodness' sake. Just snuggle up close and hold me. Let's watch the waves together," Mae replied, grabbing him by the hand.

She knew the look in her husband's eyes when he implied that he wanted to be close. In a lot of ways, she loved it, and only pretended to put up a fuss just to keep him in line. It was their form of playing a little hard to get, and he loved it just as much as she did.

"You can't blame me for trying. You are a beautiful woman, you know. Besides, there's something about being out here in this fresh air with very few people around that makes me want to act like a teenager, playing hooky from school, just so he can spend some time with his girlfriend," he said.

"Jonathan Middleton, you just celebrated your sixty-sixth birthday right before Thanksgiving. Those teenage years are long gone, my dear... long gone." She laughed.

"That may be, but my desire for you is here to stay. I love you, Mae."

Mae moved a hair of his in place while she snuggled up closer, dreaming of their next romantic getaway. Prior to their marriage, she never considered herself to be romantic, but little by little,

Jonathan was helping her to discover another side of herself.

"I have a perfect idea for our next date night," she said.

"What's that?"

"How about we prepare our boat for a quick trip up to Annapolis? We can crank up the heat and sail... maybe even have dinner and go see the Christmas lights," Mae said.

"I thought you wanted to give the boat a rest for the winter. What changed your mind?"

"Perhaps the customers at Lighthouse Tours. They're not allowing the cooler temperatures to get in their way. Why should we?"

"Mae, I'm proud of you. You've come a long way from where you used to be when we first met."

"Do you think?" She winked at him.

"Oh, I know it."

He placed his lips firmly on her cheek and then passed her their dessert.

"So, is there anything special that you want for Christmas... maybe jewelry, clothing, or a new trinket for your garden?"

"Jonathan, you know I don't need anything. I have you, my daughter Lily, her husband, and my grandbabies coming for Christmas. What more could I ask for?"

"I figured you would say such a thing, but you

know it's not always about what you need. There isn't one item that you have in mind, Mae?"

"Not one. Well... except for-"

She leaned over, whispering something in his ear to make him smile like a Cheshire Cat.

"Now that, I can start working on tonight. Come here. I love you, honey," he said, laughing so hard he made his belly jiggle.

Clara's sister, Agnes, pressed through the crowd, making her way to a booth for an afternoon meal at the café. It was her first day off in a while since taking a restaurant job north of the island. She was ready to sit down with her laptop and conduct some research, yet intrigued by the handsome singer, sitting in the corner, pulling on the strings of his guitar.

"Well, well, well... look who we have here. Agnes, is that you?" Mack asked, greeting her in a Santa Claus hat.

"Yes, it's me, in the flesh. How are you, Mackenzie?"

"I'm great. Even better now that you're here. It's so good to see you."

"Likewise. I've been so busy working at the Seafood Shack, I almost forgot what it was like to treat myself to a nice hot meal."

"Well, you came to the right place. Today we

have a special treat for our customers. Mrs. Dudley's grandson, Clay, is in town visiting her for the month of December. He's a singer. The ladies of Solomons Island absolutely adore him." She giggled.

"I can see why. He's good looking and definitely has a pleasant set of lungs on him," Agnes replied.

"Yes, it's a treat to have him here for the holidays. He usually comes in during our busiest times and lulls the crowd with a Christmas rendition or two. He makes some of the old housewives forget they're married for at least an hour or more." Mack laughed.

She then tapped Agnes on the arm, letting her in on a secret.

"Don't look now, but Mrs. Dudley is the woman sitting over by the jukebox, wearing red. She's a regular. Love the woman to death, I really do, but she's notorious for always asking for the Monday special on the wrong day of the week. It's getting to the point where Chef Harold just makes it anyway to keep her happy. Thank God he has a good sense of humor." Mack continued to chuckle.

"I'll bet."

"You know, you and Clara are like two birds of a feather. Back when she was job hunting, she used to come in here with her laptop and research, just like you. What's so important that it can't wait until after you enjoy your food?" she asked.

"My food truck business. I'm making substantial progress with applying for the proper licensing and doing all that I can, getting my ducks in a row to open up shop this summer."

"Wow. I had no idea. Clara didn't mention a thing. What about your job at the Seafood Shack? Isn't it still rather new?"

Agnes smiled enthusiastically, willing to share her plans.

"Yes, I'm planning on keeping my job in the beginning. I figured I could work out a schedule that allowed me to work the truck on certain days while still collecting a steady paycheck at the restaurant. I come across people who do it all the time. Hopefully, the transition will go just as smoothly for me. Don't worry. I have no intentions of parking near the café. I know how special your customers are to you," she replied.

"The thought didn't even cross my mind. Instead, I was thinking if there's any way I can be resourceful, hopefully you would let me know. Maybe someone like Chef Harold could help with planning your menu, or I can put a few calls in to some of my friends over at the county office. Either way, you have a lot of help around here. All you have to do is ask."

"Thank you, Mackenzie. I appreciate that." Agnes smiled.

"Sure, hun. Any sister of Clara's is a sister of mine as well. I like the way you two have been able to make amends, and how you're building a solid foundation for yourself here in Solomons. You should be proud of yourself. I know Clara is proud of you."

"Thanks. I'm sure you already know I didn't arrive here under the best circumstances. Honestly, I wouldn't be surprised if I didn't have a bad reputation around the island. It's not often you hear about a sister dating her sister's ex-husband."

Mack cut her off before she could go any further. Partially being protective of Agnes' past, the other part of her strongly believing in the spirit of grace and forgiveness.

"Stop right there, Agnes. Respectfully, you don't owe an explanation to anyone. Whatever happened between you and Clara is for you to know... and trust me when I tell you... no one around this island is talking about you in that way. If they were, I'd hear about it, right here at the café. Besides, that's not what Solomons is about," Mack said, taking a brief seat across from Agnes as she laid down her menu.

"Do you want to know what these people talk about the most?" She continued.

"What?"

"Sailing their boats, the beach, crab... oh... and occasionally, you'll get a few who like to go hunting north of the island, bringing back enough stories to make you question whether you want to continue to eat meat." She chuckled.

Mack continued. "Most important of all, we're all about family and maintaining great friendships out here, like the one I have with Clara. In my opinion, if you know even a little about any of those topics, you and your business are going to do well out here. You wait and see."

"Thank you, Mack, I appreciate it." Agnes smiled, wiping a tear from her eye.

"You bet. Now, for the reason you came here, which is to eat. Here's our menu. I'll let you listen to Clay play his guitar while I grab a glass of water for your table. Glance over the options, and I'll be right back to take your order." Mack got up and patted Agnes on the shoulder, feeling good about their little chat.

CHAPTER 7

As Clara and Mike sat in the waiting area, they could hear Mayor Thompson arguing on the other side of his office door. Brenda, his secretary, was gracious to offer coffee and oatmeal cookies, but after his second round of caffeine, Mike was still anxious about the day's events and was ready to leave.

Across the street from the mayor's office was a beautiful view of the island's gazebo. An area where everyone usually gathered for the annual Christmas tree lighting and caroling. Her eyes remained focused on the view, wondering where all the wreaths and holiday decorations were.

Mike broke her trend of thought. "Brenda, thank you for the coffee and cookies, but I think we may need to reschedule our meeting. It sounds like Mayor

Thompson is really busy, and Clara and I really should get on with our day," he said.

Just then, Mayor Thompson apologetically emerged from his office door.

"Please don't leave. Mike, I'm so sorry for the delay. It's been one heck of a day fighting tooth and nail with these contractors. Please... if you can spare just a little more time, I'd really appreciate it," he said.

"Sure, I get it. We've had an interesting day ourselves," Mike said, gesturing toward Clara.

"Hi, Mayor Thompson. It's nice to see you," she said, extending her hand.

"No formalities, Clara. To you and Mike, it's Sylvester. Please, step into my office and make yourselves comfortable."

Inside his office were a ton of awards and recognitions hanging on the wall. In the bookcase behind his chair were photos of his wife and three grown sons.

"Mae shared with us you had an urgent matter you wanted to meet about," Clara said.

Once comfortably situated, Sylvester began to explain.

"I might as well cut right to the chase. Solomons Island desperately needs someone to organize Christmas Nights. I don't know how we dropped the ball on this, but this year all the contractors' rates have gone through the roof, far superseding our budget. The street lamps need decorating, the gazebo is bare, we don't have a boat parade, and the entire boardwalk should be lit by now-"

He paused to catch his breath.

"We normally pull out all the stops, making this a spectacular time not only for the residents, but for the tourists who will come to visit and spend money. The shops on the island have come to expect the additional revenue. Our finance department should've been on top of this back when it was warm outside. If we don't get our act together soon, we're going to blow it for everybody," he said.

"Yikes, that explains things. We've been wondering what was going on," Clara said.

"Right. You can only imagine the heat I'm going to feel if I don't find a way to pull this off. I've gone as far as taking the entire matter into my hands, as if I don't already have enough to do as mayor. The only problem is... I've got nothing. My well of ideas is drying up."

"Sylvester, this doesn't sound good, and I'm sure you're feeling the pressure, but-" Mike paused, feeling uncertain about how he should say what he was thinking.

"What does this have to do with you and Clara?" Sylvester asked.

Clara and Mike glanced at each other, then locked eyes with him again.

"Well... yes. Please don't take it the way it sounds," Mike said.

"No, no. I totally understand. To be honest, I called this meeting with you because I desperately need your help," he replied.

Mike let out a little laughter, catching on to where Mayor Thompson was going with his request.

"You want our help? Sylvester, you can't be serious. I mean... yes, we do a pretty decent job at decorating our storefront, but there's a big difference between making a window look good versus professionally decorating an entire street that runs through the center of the island."

Clara remained silent but nodded along in agreement.

"There's more to it than just the decorating. Although, I need your help with that as well. We need somebody to run our boat parade. You and I talked about doing something grand for the fourth, but it never came together. This time we desperately need you, Mike... the island needs you. Our local businesses need your help. You of all people know what tourists can do for business."

"Yeah, about that. You know, in most cases, I'd be happy to throw something together. I really would. But, I'm in a bind of my own, and quite frankly I'm having a hard time seeing my way out of it," Mike said, reaching into his back pocket, pulling out a piece of paper.

He opened the paper and placed it on Sylvester's desk.

"What's this?"

"I was hoping you could tell me. At this point, you're my last resort. A messenger who delivered a notice from the clerk's office greeted me earlier today with that envelope. I almost couldn't believe my eyes when I read the thirty-day notice, threatening to confiscate all my equipment, if it's not removed from the portion of the dock that extends behind the vacant store next to me."

"Why would you have to remove equipment from a dock that belongs to you?" Sylvester asked.

"Funny... I asked the same question when I went marching into the clerk's office. I walked in confidently with my papers in hand, ready to show them my deed. Only problem, as they so graciously pointed out, is the new deed doesn't include the correct square footage of the dock as it once was written in the previous deed that my old partner Kenny and I shared. Apparently, last year when I completely took over the business and ended my partnership, I signed documents agreeing to less property than I previously had. We've always operated Lighthouse Tours using the entire dock. Even if my clients don't board the boats down there, I have always used the space for extra boat storage. The cleaners know it and have never used the space, and neither did the jeweler when he was here," Mike said, sounding frustrated.

Clara reached out her hand and gently placed it

on Mike's arm. He looked her way and relaxed his posture, signaling for her to continue.

"Sylvester, I think what Mike is trying to say is this has taken us both by surprise. The property setup will immediately impact Lighthouse Tours and its livelihood in a negative way."

"Not if I have anything to do with it," Sylvester replied.

Clara let out a sigh.

"That's what we were hoping you would say, because our hands are really tied at this point. To make matters worse, we have tough competition trying to slither their way into the store space next door to us. The guy goes by the name of Logan Woods. He operates a large boating company and marina out of Virginia. His company easily has a net worth in the millions," she said and then looked at Mike to take it from there.

Mike continued. "He tried to make me an offer to buy out Lighthouse Tours that had a lot of zeros behind it. But, when I held fast and told him I wasn't interested-"

Clara tag teamed with Mike, finishing his sentence. "He made it known he was going to do business here in Solomons, offering the locals storage, tours... the full array of what we offer and then some. This means he fully plans on becoming the next best boating company in Solomons and our new competition," she said.

Clara and Mike allowed their arms to drop in between their chairs, locking fingers, supporting one another.

"No one ever likes it when the big dogs move into town, but in this case, the timing couldn't be worse. So, while I'd love to help, Sylvester... I don't know that I'm your guy. At least not this time around," Mike said.

Sylvester glanced over the details of the notice, then tossed the paper down on his desk.

"Something here isn't adding up. The island isn't in the business of taking property back from its rightful owners, so rest easy knowing that I will do all that I can to get this resolved asap. If I have to, I'll call the realtor of the property next door, every owner that's ever done business along the dock, and anyone else I need to call to set the record straight. But for now, my gut tells me I need to start right here with the clerk's office and see what I can find out," Sylvester said.

"I'd appreciate it. Lighthouse Tours is our bread and butter. Not just us, but a list of faithful employees as well. As it is, we're already going to have a tough time with competition, even when the property issue is fixed. This guy is talking about purchasing the warehouse and really setting up shop. That's a problem in my book," Mike replied.

"I understand where you're coming from, but

perhaps there's a way the folks of Solomons Island can help."

"How? This is so much bigger than you think. I refuse to give in and sell my business because I've worked too hard for it. Yet, no one has the budget to compete with this guy. He went as far as sending out a survey to people here on the island, and they expressed an interest in having a larger boat storage facility. You know that involves shrink wrap, space, you name it... all the things I can't provide right now because I don't have the space. We're operating tours at max capacity, we finally expanded into boat rentals, but this... this I can't do without the space and the capital to put down on the warehouse," Mike responded.

Sylvester leaned in closer, resting his forearms on his desk.

"Mike, whose business do you think the people would much rather support? Lighthouse Tours... a name known and trusted... owned by one of Solomons very own, Mike Sanders... or some big shot outsider who could potentially turn this place into something it's not?" Sylvester asked.

"I would hope Lighthouse Tours," he responded.

Clara turned and faced Mike.

"Hope? The people who support Lighthouse Tours love you. So much that they spread the word to others far and near, Mike."

"My point exactly, which is why I see an opportunity here, if you will hear me out," Sylvester said.

He stood up and paced over to his window, peering out of the blinds.

"Like I said earlier, I'll look into the concern with your deed and have the problem resolved before the end of the week. I'm almost certain it's an error that can be fixed. Even if by some chance the new deed is justified, we'll get an addendum in motion asap. As for Christmas Nights, I'd like for you to think long and hard about my request. We've already ordered all the wreaths and garland for the street lamps, gazebo, the boardwalk, and we can even offer to help decorate the store fronts down Main Street. The shipment should be here on Friday. To make it extra special this year, we want all of main street to be lined with candle lanterns, giving our visitors a delightful experience as they walk the streets and shop. We're getting the word out to everyone who does business on Main Street that illuminated decorations are a must. As a bonus, all boat owners will be invited to decorate their boats with Christmas lights and join in the parade, hopefully led by one of our faithful employees of Lighthouse Tours-"

"But-" Mike interrupted.

"Hear me out. I was thinking if you could leave the parade up to Jonathan, Mae... maybe even Brody, then it would give you time to focus on organizing the concert for the Christmas tree lighting ceremony at the gazebo."

Clara's mouth dropped open.

"Concert? What happened to the carolers?" she asked.

"We can still utilize them to sing outside of the shops and on the steps of the chapel. However, we have a young man in town who's sure to draw in a large crowd. He's a popular singer, known for playing the guitar, and has a way about him that leaves the crowd begging for more. He's Mrs. Dudley's grandson, and since she owes me a favor, I plan on putting in a special request to have him sing the night of the tree lighting."

Sylvester walked around to the front of the desk, leaning back and scratching his chin as if he was on to something.

"The idea just hit me like a ton of bricks... wouldn't it be nice if we turned this event into a tree lighting ceremony and benefit concert to help Lighthouse Tours purchase the warehouse? It would benefit the people of Solomons Island, giving them what they want. It would definitely keep your business up and running, and most important of all, it would encourage this guy Woods to take his business elsewhere. Think about it. What kind of operation is he really going to run if he doesn't have the dock or the warehouse?" Sylvester said, raising his eyebrows.

Clara spoke first. "In an ideal world, it makes perfect sense. We would do something good for Solomons by setting things up for Christmas Nights... this way the store owners wouldn't lose revenue this year-" she said.

"Right, and Solomons would do something in return for us, which ultimately still benefits them because they would have the boat storage they need. But, how in the world could we pull this together with such short notice?" Mike asked.

They both stared at Sylvester.

"Leave it up to my office to get the word out. We'll print fliers and pass them out by hand if we have to. We'll update our website and notify the newspaper and the local news. Every business owner on Main Street will be made aware of the protocol for decorations. I'll even speak with Mrs. Dudley's grandson today. All we need you to do is round up a crew to help with decorations, get a few of your folks over at Lighthouse Tours to make plans for the boat parade, and have everything in place by next Saturday, the eleventh... the night of the tree lighting," he said.

"Next Saturday? You're joking, right?" Mike asked.

Sylvester opened his mouth, letting out a hardy laughter.

"I wish I was joking. I meant it when I told you I was in a real bind with these contractors. And from what I can tell, it looks like you're in a bind of your own. Why not work together and make this the greatest Christmas Solomons has ever had? If we join forces, we could kill two birds-"

"With one stone... I got it. This isn't necessarily a bad idea, but one week is still a tall order," Mike said.

"Babe, we can round up everyone and get all hands on deck to help make it happen. Especially once they learn it's for a good cause. We got this. I really think we can pull it off. Plus, it will be just in time for your folks to arrive. Wouldn't it be nice to have them be a part of such a beautiful event?" Clara smiled.

"I didn't think of it that way," Mike replied, returning his gaze back to the mayor.

So... does that mean we have a deal?" Sylvester asked.

Mike noticed a small snow globe resting on Sylvester's desk. Inside was the architectural design of the gazebo and the dock, displaying the center of town with people passing by. He picked up the globe and gave it a hearty shake, smiling at the sight of the snowflakes whirling around.

"Count me in," he said and shook Sylvester's hand, making it official.

CHAPTER 8

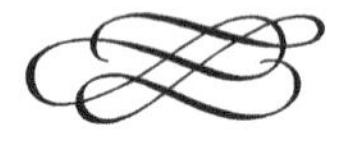

"Stephanie, what do you say to Brody for helping us to pick out our tree?" Mackenzie asked.

"Thank you, Brody. This is the best tree we've ever had. Mom usually picks out a small one because she can't carry the big ones on her own," she replied.

"I'm glad you like it. Now, if you get the star, then I can lift you up so you can place it at the top."

Stephanie ran over to the box of decorations, excitedly picking out the star and returning for the grand finale.

"All right, now I'm going to hoist you up on the count of three. Place the star right at the top and then we'll ask mom to plug in the tree. On the count of three, ready?"

"I think so," she said.

"One... two... three." Brody grunted, lifting her up.

Stephanie was tall for her age. In her second-grade class, she outranked the height of most of the other kids, but thankfully was sweet enough not to use it against the others. As soon as Mackenzie plugged in the lights, the tree sparkled from the star all the way to the last ornament hanging at the bottom.

"The tree is absolutely beautiful." Mack gasped, holding her hands to her mouth.

"It is breathtaking. Now I know who to call should I need help with my decorations over at my place," Brody said.

"We'd be happy to help you, Brody. It's the least we can do since you helped us," Stephanie said.

"Thanks, Steph. The sad part is I normally go with a three-foot tree that sits in the middle of my dinette table. Nothing fancy, but should I ever decide to spice things up, your name is at the top of my list," he said.

"Thanks," Stephanie said, while trying to stifle a yawn.

"There it is... the first yawn of the evening. I figured it was only a matter of time. Especially since we stayed out later than usual, picking out a tree." Mack teased.

"But, Mommy..."

"No buts, young lady. We had a deal. You have

your Christmas tree and it's fully decorated, thanks to Brody. Now it's time for you to do your part, which is march right to the back, wash your face, and brush your teeth. After that..."

"I know, head straight to bed," Stephanie said in a somber voice.

"Can I at least grab a chocolate chip cookie to go? I promise I'll brush as soon as I finish," Stephanie asked.

"Yes, love. But first-" Mack signaled toward Brody.

Stephanie gave him a big teddy bear hug, holding on for several moments before letting go.

"Are you really happy with the tree?" he asked in a low voice.

She nodded her head yes.

"Good, that makes me happy." Brody smiled.

Stephanie then held her hand up to Brody's ear. "My Christmas wish is to have a dad just like you someday," she whispered.

"Aww, you're melting my heart, kiddo."

She gave him a quick kiss on the cheek, then hugged her mother, and skipped off, making a pit stop at the cookie jar before saying goodnight.

Brody sniffled, and then quickly shifted, trying to hide his emotions.

"Whatever that was about, she must've struck a chord. Are you okay?" Mackenzie asked.

"Me? Yeah... I just have a little tickle in my throat, that's all."

"Sure, you do. Why don't you come sit with me until your so-called tickle goes away?" She giggled, then sat on the couch, making room for him to join her.

"Seriously, I think my allergies are kicking in." He smiled, clearing his throat.

"Brody, since when do you have allergies?"

"Okay, okay. You got me. It's not my fault, though. That girl of yours is starting to have an effect on my heart. She's so precious, which makes it even harder to understand why her father refuses to be a constant staple in her life," he said.

"Believe me, I know firsthand what you mean. But it's his fault that he's missing out. One day he'll soon come to regret it... hopefully even wake up to the error of his ways... and if not, at least Steph and I still have each other. Our dynamic has worked for this long. I don't see why it would fail now."

"It won't. You two make a strong team. If you don't mind me asking, has he at least made contact so he can see her for the holidays?" Brody said.

"Nope. The sad part is, she's so used to it she hasn't even asked."

"Wow," he replied.

"Yep, my sentiments exactly... and just so you know, I would never expect you to take his place, but what you did for her tonight truly made her day. Even the plans you're making for Friday, with the bonfire and all... she is so looking forward to it. Thank you, Brody. From the bottom of our hearts," Mack said.

Toward the back of the apartment, she could hear Stephanie turning off the water in the bathroom.

"Stephanie, did you brush good?" she yelled.

"Yes, Mom. Can I listen to my music to help me fall asleep?"

"Only the selections from your nighttime playlist. Ten minutes max. Anything after that you'll have to count sheep. I'll come tuck you in right after Brody leaves," Mack said.

"Okay."

"That girl will stall until midnight if I let her. Anything to stay up a few more minutes," she whispered.

Brody laughed and then gazed into her eyes, carefully placing a hand on her cheek.

"What's on your mind?" Mack asked.

"You. I was just sitting here thinking, there's no place I'd rather be right now than with you."

Mack held up one finger, motioning for him to wait as she listened to the sound of Stephanie's door closing. Once the first song started to play, she nestled closer to him.

"Kiss me," she said.

He checked over her shoulders, then cautiously

planted his warm lips on hers long enough to feel like a tease.

"Kiss me, again... and this time don't stop."

He did, causing her stomach to flutter as they held each other by the Christmas tree.

On Wednesday morning, Mike held an impromptu meeting at Lighthouse Tours. Members of his staff gathered in the conference room, welcoming Mackenzie, an added guest. All it took was a brief phone call from Clara to get her involved. She offered support from the café staff and was willing to do whatever she could to help Lighthouse Tours.

"Okay, everyone, I'm going to cut straight to the chase. First, I'd like to welcome Mackenzie to our meeting this morning. Clara and I were most appreciative when she accepted the invitation to join us."

Everyone smiled, some looking a little perplexed as to why she was there, but welcomed her just the same.

Mike continued.

"Most of you already know about the concern with the dock. Thankfully, first thing this morning, I received a call from Mayor Thompson directly. He explained that after they did some digging around over at the clerk's office, they discovered an error was made by the person who drew up the new papers when I became the sole owner of the company. To put it simply, the dock is and will always be a part of this property-"

Cheers and whistles interrupted him from everyone across the room.

"Thank you. Believe me, I share the same sentiments. My biggest takeaway is always double check anything that requires your signature. As a businessman, I should've known better, but thankfully the issue was quickly resolved. With that behind us, now we can move on to the second hurtle."

"Another hurtle?" Mae sighed.

"Yes, one that has the potential to be just as damaging to the company if we don't do something about it right away," he replied.

"Mike, I don't know how many hiccups we can take in one week," Brody responded.

"Amen. I completely agree, but it's the hand we're being dealt, Brody. The best thing we can do is rally together and see if we can put an end to this mess before it gets any further out of hand."

"An end to what mess?" Tommy asked.

"A competitor by the name of The Virginia Boating Company is threatening to bring its business here to Solomons Island. The owner's name is Logan Woods. He runs a full-service operation offering much more than tours and rentals... and his current business is making the kind of money that could pretty much run us off the island."

"So, you're talking about one of those big chain types?" Jonathan asked.

"Yep, except he's not a chain. He commands that kind of volume all on his own, and from what I can tell, he's looking to further expand. My introduction to Logan came in the form of an offer to buy out Lighthouse Tours — it was an offer I declined, of course. All it took was one brief conversation to let me know this guy was all about the money, caring nothing about the people of the island. I'm sure Clara could tell you even more as she met him face to face and found out the inside scoop on his interest in the property next door."

Mike signaled Clara to continue.

"Yes, I'm afraid it's true. Logan is certainly more of an enemy rather than an ally, and definitely not someone we would want to welcome to the island, especially not next door," she said.

"Next door, as in right next to Lighthouse Tours?" Jonathan asked, practically gasping at the news.

"Yes. You can only imagine how panicked it made me feel to have this going on in conjunction with the dock issue. Even with that being resolved, Woods claims he surveyed the people of Solomons Island, and says they all want a larger storage facility for their boat — something he can easily deliver and threatened to do so if he purchases the warehouse," Mike said.

"The warehouse, too? You gotta be kidding me," Brody said, then looked over at Mackenzie as if searching for answers.

"Trust me when I tell you, man... there's no kidding going on here at all. Logan Woods is serious, which means we all have to be smart about this," Mike responded.

"Well, I just want you to know that if I ever received a survey from another boating company, I would probably throw it in the trash," Mae said.

"I did receive it, but I never took it seriously. I just threw it in my junk mail pile with plans to shred it whenever I got around to it. I can bring it in if you'd like," Tommy said.

"Thanks, Tommy, but at this point, we shouldn't get caught up in the survey. Obviously, enough people on the island responded, and now it's our job to give them an opportunity to make a choice. We've been here providing service to the area for years now. I was thinking maybe we can paint a picture for them, showing them what we can provide for the island with their help. But, it all boils down to one thing... do the people of Solomons Island really want a big flashy company taking over and changing the dynamic of our quaint beach community? That's what will happen if Logan Woods starts a business here. Or do their hearts lie with Lighthouse Tours? And are they willing to trust us to deliver what they want while maintaining the integrity of the island?

We certainly don't have the capital to just purchase the warehouse on a whim. I still have our office in North Beach to think about. Therefore, if the people really want us to stay, this has to be their decision. All we're going to do is present them with an option to help move things in the right direction. The rest is up to the community."

The room fell silent for a moment. Most sat with serious expressions on their faces.

"What kind of option?"

Mike and Clara both looked at Mackenzie.

"Well, good folks, that's where Lighthouse Tours and the café can form a partnership. It's been brought to my attention that as of this moment, Solomons Island has absolutely no plans in place for Christmas Nights... isn't that right, Clara?" Mackenzie asked in a jovial voice.

"It certainly is," Clara replied.

"Why do you two seem so happy about such a terrible thing?" Mae asked.

"We're happy because Mayor Thompson has officially given us the charge to organize the decorations, the Christmas tree lighting, a boat parade, and drumroll please..." Clara said, excitedly sitting on the edge of her seat.

Everyone gave her a blank stare.

"Okay, perhaps no drum roll... but we're excited to announce that Mrs. Dudley's grandson, Clay, has agreed to put on a concert for the tree lighting ceremony at the gazebo. This will not only attract even more tourists to support the local businesses but... Mike, why don't you tell them," she said, nodding his way.

"A portion of the proceeds from that night, plus donations accepted until the end of the month, will go toward purchasing the warehouse for the additional boat storage they've been requesting. This will give the people of Solomons Island the additional storage they need and keep our businesses one hundred percent locally owned. In all honesty, I was hesitant at first, thinking this would be too much of an undertaking. But, if nothing else, Solomons Island is about to have the best Christmas Nights experience they've ever had, and all the local shops are about to bring in more revenue for the holidays than ever before. That alone is enough for me," Mike said.

"It sounds like a marvelous idea, but can we really pull this off? Decorating the town and putting on a boat parade is no easy task," Jonathan said.

Mackenzie hopped out of her chair and walked around to the center of the room.

"That's where all of us come in. Picture this. Some of us can take charge of the fliers... it can say something like 'Christmas Nights Tree Lighting and Benefit Concert: Starring Clay Nathan, country singer extraordinaire, performing Christmas hits and a few personal favorites for the Christmas Nights Tree Lighting Ceremony. Come ready to visit the shops, see the Christmas lights, and help by bringing your donations so our very own Lighthouse Tours can provide boat storage for the residents of Solomons Island'. It may be a bit wordy, but you get the idea," she said, holding her hands in the air as if she were reading a billboard.

Mike approved, giving her the thumbs up.

"Then there's more. Dakota and I can reach out to all the store owners on Main Street, organizing the specific days they can come to pick up their illuminated candles for their windows. Josh can round up a bunch of his buddies to handle decorating the street lamps and the gazebo." Mackenzie continued.

Jonathan gladly jumped in.

"I can take on the task of organizing the boat parade. What do you say we decorate each boat a different color? Or maybe one can be all green, another white, then red... and so on and so forth. We could line up the entire fleet right up to the area where the gazebo is. Maybe even have a few of the local college kids help us sail the boats and dress up as Santa Claus," he said.

"That would be amazing. Great idea," Mike said.

"I'm happy to help Jonathan, and I can put in some foot work in the evening to help pick out a tree for the gazebo. I know two special ladies who'd probably be very interested in heading to the tree farm with me. We can even measure just to be sure," Brody said, winking at Mackenzie.

She giggled excitedly at the idea.

"We'd love to join you, sweetheart," she said, completely forgetting she had an audience.

Mackenzie continued. "Eh em. Where were we? Oh, yes. This just leaves us with figuring out who's going to ensure the chapel is decorated, who's going to see to it that all storefronts are ready within the allotted time, and who's going to organize people in shifts who can collect donations during the concert and stand at various posts throughout Main Street as people shop. We'll need plenty of volunteers who would take shifts leading up to Christmas Eve," Mackenzie said.

"Yikes, that might be our downfall. People will swarm the streets in droves. Do you think we can gather enough volunteers?" Mae asked.

"Not only do I think it... I know it's possible. Leave that up to me. I'll even reach out to our North Beach staff and elicit their help as well," Mike said.

"Fantastic. That does it. It sounds like we have ourselves a plan. I'm just going to create a spreadsheet to make sure we stay on track of who's doing what. Technically phase one, which is the decorations, tree lighting, boat parade, and concert need to happen by the eleventh. That's one week from this Saturday, and we must adhere to the schedule. Clay said he'd handle everything pertaining to audio and sound, so we're covered there," Clara said.

"That's correct. I'll bet Jan from North Beach

would help organize the volunteers. You two work well together, and both have a knack for checklists and spreadsheets," Mike said.

"Perfect." Clara agreed.

"Oh, and let's not forget Josh. That man is a worker bee. We can give him an extra task. He'd be happy to help out," Mackenzie offered.

"Thanks, Mack," Mike said.

He then sat back in his chair, scratching his chin for a moment.

"There's one more thing that comes to mind if we're going to do this thing right. Somewhere on the flier, we need to let the people know that all future earnings from the warehouse will cover the cost of operation, the employees, and a percentage will go back to the community for Christmas Nights every year. I'm invested in this island, and I think it's only fair that we come up with a way to celebrate the season like this for years to come," Mike said.

"That's the spirit... and that's also the man this island has come to know and love," Clara replied.

"Yeah, Mike. At this rate, you're offering something Logan Woods can't buy. You have one-hundred and ten percent of my support for anything you need. Just say the word," Jonathan said.

"That makes two of us." Mae joined in, while locking hands with Jonathan.

Tommy, Brody, and Mackenzie nodded in agreement.

"Well, in that case, we've got work to do. We'll touch base with everyone at the start of each day, making sure we're on track with our assigned tasks. No matter the outcome, I appreciate you and all that you do for Lighthouse Tours. Unless anybody has anything further to add, our meeting is adjourned."

Clara returned to the conference room, placing two mugs of hot chocolate on the table, one next to Mike's laptop, and the other in between her hands, keeping them warm.

"Mike, I'm so proud of you. Your idea about giving back to Solomons every year was genius, and with everybody's help, there's no way we can't pull this off. Once I tell Agnes, I'll bet she'll want to join in as well."

"That would be awesome. The more hands, the better. I honestly don't know how to feel right now. The more I process the whole thing, I'm extremely nervous and excited all at the same time. During the meeting I quietly wondered if I'd lost my mind, considering how much there is to do," he said.

"Ha, I know the feeling. But, even if we have to pull an all nighter or two... I believe the result is going to be amazing. I'd venture as far as saying, even dreamy, with the main strip of the island being illuminated in Christmas lights. People will come from miles to drive and see the sights," she responded, placing her hand over his.

"Clara, what would I do without you? I don't think you understand how much my life has changed for the better with you in it... and if all this wasn't enough, in a couple of weeks, I'll finally have the pleasure of having you and my parents together in the same room," he said.

"I feel the same way about you, love, but truthfully the latter part freaks me out."

"Oh, no. Please don't tell me you're going to start worrying about what my parents will think of you again," he said.

"No... no... no... I'm past that now. I'm talking about being ready for their arrival. I'm sure you'll make your place as comfortable as possible, and I'll make sure I load up on extra groceries if you want to bring them over to the house for dinner. But what about their Christmas gifts?"

"There's not a thing that we can't order and have sent to the house. I'll handle that part. Maybe you can find something for the staff?" he asked, while staring at a potential cost analysis for purchasing the warehouse.

Clara reached over and closed his laptop to get his undivided attention.

"Mike Sanders, I'm not kicking off the gift giving tradition with your parents by ordering some quick and thoughtless gift online. I can already see it now...

a tie, a robe, or a foot massager just won't do. If you want to make this special, and from the two of us, then the gifts have to be personal. It can't be something they'll want to re-gift when they get back home." She emphasized.

"I didn't realize you'd be so passionate about it. How about I call them and discretely find a way to come up with a few ideas?"

"That sounds more like it." She smiled.

"Good. Now on to the immediate task at hand. I need to put in a call to Dylan, the owner of the warehouse, and make him aware of our intentions. Maybe you can take a ride with me. The old warehouse has been sitting on the market for almost a year now. I heard he's been pretty firm on his asking price and not willing to budge. I'm almost certain it's the reason the place hasn't sold. I don't want to get ahead of myself, but if Solomons is on board with supporting this whole thing, then maybe he'd be willing to work with me on the price. I figure there's no harm in trying anyway."

"That's a great idea. Do you want me to look up his info and try to get him on the phone for you?" Clara said.

"Yes, please. But, before you do, I need something really important."

"What's that?"

"You," he said, closing his eyes and puckering up.

She indulged him for a little while and then retreated to the door.

"I'm walking away now so we can get something accomplished." She teased.

With the door almost closed, she poked her head back in with a final thought.

"I almost forgot to mention that Agnes and I are cooking dinner tonight. You're more than welcome to come by and grab a bite," she said.

"I wish I could, but I was thinking tonight I'd dedicate several hours to laying out a blueprint for everyone to follow."

"Oh, well, in that case, we can bring the food to you. I'm sure Agnes won't mind helping me pack up some food to go. There's one more thing before I forget... remember the sweet couple who let me hang out at their store in Huntingtown?" she asked.

"Yeah, met them the night you and Agnes had a disagreement and your car ran out of gas."

"That's the couple... I was thinking of inviting them down for Christmas Nights. We always said we would have them down for a tour. Why not invite them to ride one of the boats for the parade? You never know, maybe they can even spread the word around their community and bring a few friends," she said.

"I like the way you think, Clara Covington... I like the way you think."

CHAPTER 9

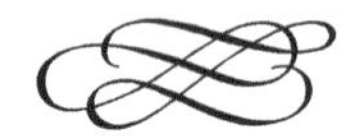

Mae lay in bed staring at the ceiling while Jonathan tossed and turned. He'd been wrestling with the sheets for what seemed like an hour, keeping her wide awake.

"Jonathan, maybe you could fall asleep if you weren't so overheated, sweetheart. I never understood how you could wear a full set of flannel pajamas to bed in the first place." She complained.

"It's not the pajamas, Mae. I wear these every year around Christmas and have always slept like a baby."

"Oh. Well, did you watch too much of the late night news? It leaves a lasting impression right before you go to bed, you know. They rarely have anything positive to say. I've even had nightmares every now and again," she said.

"No, Mae. I caught the weather and that's about it."

He threw the covers off and rolled over, joining Mae in a staring contest.

"Then what's keeping you up tonight? Something has to be on your mind. You're normally snoring so loud, I have to fight the temptation to smack you with a pillow." She laughed.

"Very funny, Mae. Very funny."

She positioned herself to face Jonathan, placing her hand on his arm.

"Seriously, Jonathan. Is everything okay? You don't seem like yourself tonight."

He sighed.

"I spoke to the doctor this afternoon. He said my blood work came back, showing my sugar levels were high — I think he used the words pre-diabetic. He gave me a list of things to do before I come back for my next physical. Not exactly the kind of news I wanted to hear right before the holidays."

"Pre-diabetic? Oh, for goodness' sake. Not with the way we eat. You should've asked him if he had the right file. You have always been a perfect picture of health, drinking your water, and eating your vegetables every single day, and only enjoying an occasional cookie or slice of cake."

"Mae." He chuckled. "I thank you for your vote of confidence in me, but if the doctor sees something in his report, I'd like to think he knows what he's talking about. I'm just trying to stay level-headed about it. I wasn't even going to say anything until Christmas Nights was behind us. But, then I remembered the family would be here soon, and it might look odd when everyone sees me avoiding dessert altogether."

Mae reared her head back, placing her hand on her hip.

"First of all, I'm glad you decided to share something this important with me. I am your wife, you know. I'm supposed to know these things so I can be a support system for you."

She was putting on her best display of strength in front of Jonathan, but deep inside, she wondered whether her food preparation could've been a contributing factor.

She gently rested her hand on his arm, snuggling up close.

"Jonathan, do you remember the time I went in for my physical and they called, almost scaring the daylights out of me with the results?"

"I sure do. What was it again? They said something about your liver enzymes, although in the end, it turned out they really had the wrong report." He laughed.

"That's exactly how it happened. The phone call almost tore me to pieces. The people in the medical profession are more busy than they've ever been, and they, like the rest of us, sometimes make mistakes."

"I don't know, Mae. My doctor is pretty good. Your situation just happened to be a fluke."

"Did you ask them to run the blood work again? Maybe two times is a charm," she said.

"You can't just ask them to keep running tests on a whim. That's not how it works."

"Jonathan, all they have to do is draw blood again and run it through a diagnostic machine or whatever have you. What's the big deal? In my opinion, they should be sure of these things before sending people off the deep end."

"Mmm hmm."

"I'm serious, Jonathan. There's no harm in calling back and asking, and if you won't, maybe I'll just have to do it for you." She insisted.

"Oh, good grief, Mae. I love you, woman. But, you sure know how to —"

She sat up in bed. "Know how to what?"

"Nothing, dear. I'll give them a call."

"First thing in the morning?"

"I can't guarantee it will be the first thing, but I will call them. Now, can we please change the subject?" Jonathan asked in the sweetest voice he could muster up as not to cause any further trouble.

"Actually, before you started tossing around, I was lying here thinking about the boat parade. Do you think we should decorate the fleet with all white lights or mix things up a bit?" she asked.

"It doesn't matter to me. I think the people are

going to love it no matter what we do. If you want, we can go with a similar theme as we did here at the house. It looks like a winter wonderland outside. So much that I think our neighbor, Meredith, is jealous... and that's after she hired a company to do her decorations. I caught a glimpse of her reaction when I turned the lights on last night. I think I saw a few horns growing out of her head." He chuckled.

"Jonathan, you are so bad. Even though... I do think we stand a good chance at winning. I'm just waiting to see what the Zimmermans decide to do with their place. The only thing shining at their house are the porch lights at night."

"I thought you heard the news," Jonathan said.

"What news?"

"The for sale sign is going up right after we ring in the new year. The Zimmermans are getting a divorce," he replied.

"That's terrible. I knew they were going through a rough patch, but I thought surely they would press through it."

Jonathan propped both arms behind his head and crossed his legs, resting comfortably.

"Yep, sometimes it happens to the best of us. One minute things are fine, and the next-" His voice trailed off.

Jonathan's words triggered flashbacks to her first marriage. Specifically, during the first year, when the longevity of their union didn't look very promising.

She was fresh out of college and only knew the examples her mother taught her about how to be a good wife. The formula seemed to work well for her parents, but not so much for her new groom, who threatened to leave more than once.

"What do you mean 'one minute' things are fine, and the next?" she asked.

He looked at her as if he missed something.

"I didn't say anything crazy, Mae. It's not unheard of these days to attend a wedding, cheering a couple on till death do they part, only to hear a short while later they're announcing a divorce. I always wish the very best for people, but it doesn't always work out that way."

Mae flung the covers over and rose to the edge of the bed.

"I had no idea you'd be so cavalier about the union between husband and wife. That's not how it's supposed to work, Jonathan. Hitting a rough patch is no excuse to call it quits. Whatever happened to doing things the old-fashioned way, sticking it out until you make it through the hard times?" She argued.

Jonathan sat up, flipping the switch to the lamp on the nightstand beside him.

"Woman, what's gotten into you? You do realize I'm referring to the Zimmermans, right?"

"No, you said 'sometimes it happens to the best of us.' That sounded all inclusive to me," she replied.

"Mae, it was a figure of speech. I hold our marriage to the highest regard. You, of all people, should know that. I pursued you for quite some time before you finally accepted my hand in marriage. Why would I be so hasty and say or do something to throw it all away?" Jonathan said, folding his eyebrows together.

Mae grunted a little but didn't say anything further.

Before she could gather her thoughts, she felt his hands grabbing her by the waistline, tickling her till she begged for mercy.

"Jonathan, please. I can't... I can't take it," she said, laughing so hard she nearly had an accident.

Their laughter began to wind down to a lingering smile as they lay in each other's arms again.

"You're like a big kid trapped inside a grown man's body. Always stirring up mischief," Mae said.

"Hey, I have to keep you on your toes. Especially since I never know who's lying in bed with me at night. Sometimes I have to ask myself, is it Mae or her alter ego?" He teased.

She lovingly swatted at him, and he laughed, drawing her in closer.

"I owe you an apology for jumping to conclusions. I know how much of a good man you are. What you said just reminded me of a time from my previous marriage that I never want to experience with you. Jonathan, promise me, if we ever go through a rough patch that you won't threaten to quit and walk out on me. I know I can be difficult at times, but you know I don't mean any harm," she said.

"Mae Middleton. I'm committed until death do us part. Which means you'd have to kick me out and change the locks and even then... I'm still not going anywhere."

"Come here and give me some sugar," she said.

"Hold that thought." He turned off the lamp, allowing the moonlight to hover over them while falling asleep in each other's arms.

Mike pulled down a long driveway leading to the warehouse, leaving a cloud of dust trailing behind. He stopped in front of the building and looked at Clara for a reaction.

"Well, what do you think?" he asked, gazing up toward the roof and checking out the surroundings.

"Uhh. I'm not sure what to think. I'm trying my best to see past the overgrown weeds and run-down appearance. The place looks like it's in desperate need of a makeover," she said.

"It's been vacant for a while, that's all. It could use a little tlc, but don't let a few minor cosmetics fool you. The place has more than enough space, it's near the water, and it's worth way more than it looks."

"That explains why he hasn't budged on the

asking price. I'm not sure if we're biting off more than we can chew or if he needs to lower the price. Either way, I think it's going to take more than a Christmas benefit concert to come up with the down payment, Mike. We may be in over our heads," she said, skimming over the listing.

"Hold on a minute. We can't lose hope without giving this thing an earnest try. Dylan, the owner, seemed to like the idea of the warehouse being repurposed to provide boat storage, and he even gave us the okay to walk around and take a look. He said he might work with us on the price. Since we already have this place plastered all over thousands of fliers as the ideal storage space, the least we can do is get out and look," Mike said.

Clara placed the listing on the dashboard and opened the door.

"I guess you're right. It's not like we have many options on the island." She sighed.

Just as Clara and Mike got out of the jeep, a blue Ford pickup began easing down the same dirt driveway. The truck roared with the distinct sound of a diesel engine, growing louder as it approached the warehouse. When the driver came to a full halt, he tipped his hat and smiled.

"Great. If it isn't the dirt bag himself, Logan Woods. What's he doing here?" Clara asked, staring right at him.

Logan exited the vehicle and walked around, hoisting his belt in place.

"Well, if it isn't the beautiful Miss Clara Covington and her fiancé, Mr. Sanders. It's nice running into you good folks out here," Logan said.

He barely made eye contact before shifting his attention to the warehouse, giving it the once over.

"She's a beauty, isn't she?" he said, walking closer toward the front entrance.

"Yeah… listen, Logan. I'm not sure if you spoke to Dylan, the owner, but we called him and actually got his permission to be here today. Is there any chance you could give us a half hour or so? Clara and I would like to conduct a walkthrough, peacefully, if you don't mind," Mike responded.

Logan chuckled. "Great minds think alike. I also put in a call to Dylan earlier today. I think he mentioned something about you being here. But since I have to head back to Virginia this afternoon, I took it upon myself to briefly stop by. I figured the property is so big, we wouldn't be in each other's way."

"Right," Mike said, feeling slightly agitated.

He looked over at Clara, who stood with her arms folded.

"I'm not sure what Dylan shared with you, but I wouldn't invest too much energy in the warehouse if I were you. I plan on submitting an offer as soon as I get things squared away for a new office space. I would've secured one sooner, if someone hadn't sabotaged my plans for the dock behind the building on Main Street," Logan said.

"Sabotage? The dock was never for sale to begin with. It was an error made by the clerk's office, which should've been caught before the store next door was ever listed for sale," Clara said.

"Logan, the real question is, why would you ever open your business right next to mine, anyway? Where's the logic in that? It's a pretty bold move if you ask me."

Logan paced slowly over to Mike, stopping inches away.

"I'll take that as a compliment, Mike. Bold is the perfect way to describe my personality. I like to make a big splash, especially with business. Main Street is all about location, location, location. I'll go anywhere or purchase anything that will help me run a successful business," he responded, then peered over at the warehouse again.

"Here's how I see things, Mike. I tried to get you to join forces with me. By now, we could've signed a sweet deal and you could've walked away with a lot of cheddar in your bank account, but you turned me down. Once you do something like that, all bets are off with me. Now I'm your competition. It's just business. I'm sure you understand," he said sarcastically.

Mike could feel Clara standing close behind him. He thought long and cautiously about the many ways he wanted to deck Woods square in the nose but thought better of it.

"I'll tell you what, Logan. In the spirit of helping you get back to Virginia as soon as possible, how about you go inside and take a look around the warehouse first? Take all the time you need. I'll wait outside with my lady," Mike responded with a hand gesture, showing him the path to the front door.

"There's no need. This is actually my second visit. I already have an idea about how the space can be used, so you and the future Mrs. can take your tour in peace." He tipped his hat at them again, and slowly backed away, returning to his truck.

Inside, Mike was fuming, but he stood still and remained calm until Woods backed all the way out of the driveway and left.

"Mike, talk to me," Clara said, taking him by the hand.

"What else is there to say? It sounds like he's devised a master plan that will take down Lighthouse Tours, making it really difficult for us to stay in business. At this rate, we won't survive another year in Solomons."

"No — don't say that. I have to believe there's something we can do. Christmas Nights is just a week away. You know how supportive Solomons is, and you know how supportive our tourists can be around the holidays. You have to believe this will all work itself out."

"Clara, even you just said it's going to take more than a benefit concert." Mike argued.

She held her hands over Mike's cheeks.

"Call it a moment of fear or delusion. Maybe even a slip of the tongue, but we can't give up now. We've already committed to making this the most spectacular event ever. We might as well see this through until the end. A truck load of decorations will arrive first thing in the morning. I need you to stay in the game with me. Are you in?" she asked.

"I'm trying, but the last thing I need is a distraction from the likes of Logan Woods. We're talking about our livelihood, Clara. It's a big deal."

"Mike, I'm well aware of all that's at stake," she said, giving him a peck on the nose.

Then she continued.

"But as you said, we can't lose hope without giving this thing an earnest try, right?"

Mike nodded.

"You're right. Besides, maybe I can give Dylan another call to feel him out."

"That's the spirit. Now let's go inside and check out this place. If we raise enough money, the first thing we need to do is bribe a bunch of college kids to help us paint." She chuckled, brushing her hand along his back as they approached the warehouse.

CHAPTER 10

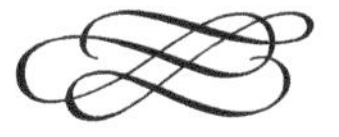

Early Friday morning, Mike arranged as many helpers as possible from Lighthouse Tours, the café, the mayor's office, and a few other businesses who were willing to pitch in. Everyone stared inside a forty-foot trailer filled with garland, wreaths, lights, and enough decorations to make their heads spin.

"Okay, folks. This is the day we've all been waiting for. The residents of Solomons, business owners, and all of last years registered guests have all received information announcing Christmas Nights as a monumental event. This year they're expecting to be wowed by the sights and sounds, and we plan to deliver."

Everyone gathered around, listening to Mike, while Clara reviewed her checklist.

"The crew at the café has been gracious enough to set up a hot chocolate station with fresh bagels, and around noon, the mayor's office will provide lunch. Our goal is to have everything finished by the end of this weekend. Mack and Brody will find a tree in the morning and do a test run on the lights. The official ceremony will take place on Friday evening with a full concert to knock their socks off and get them in the mood for shopping. Unless there are any further questions, please check in with Clara for your group assignments and let's make this island sparkle with decorations and lights."

Mike dispersed the supplies to the appropriate groups, carefully following Clara's organized chart. The garland crew took care of the street lamps, and another group focused on illuminated candles — everything was well planned.

"Have you heard from Dylan yet?" Clara asked.

"Yes, as a matter of fact. He called shortly before the trailer pulled up. Which would you like first — the good news or the bad news?" Mike asked.

"Oh goodness. Start with the bad so we can end on a pleasant note."

"Okay. The bad news, as suspected... Logan Woods expressed intentions of putting in an offer. He said he'd have his realtor send over the paperwork this week, which would leave us at square one, trying to figure out another location for boat storage."

"But Mike, there are no other locations. The

warehouse is our only option. It amazes me how no one has touched the place in over a year and now suddenly Logan is putting in an offer," she said, sounding frustrated.

Mike pulled her to the side so they could speak privately.

"Hold on a second. Remember, I said there was good news as well?" he asked.

"Yes."

"The good news is Dylan has a vested interest in making sure the warehouse remains in the family, as he put it," Mike replied.

"In the family?"

"Yes, in the Solomons family, of course. He said we all have long-standing relationships and look out for one another on the island. He'd hate to see the warehouse go to some stranger who will do more harm by bringing his big-name company to Solomons than good. Dylan has been living on the island and doing business here for decades, and the only thing he wants to see is the small business tradition carry on."

"Wow."

"I know. I told you it was good news. Of course, we're still faced with the challenge of raising the funds for a down payment... he can't just give the warehouse away. But, for now, he's willing to take it off the market to help buy us some time. As of this moment, the warehouse is no longer for sale. But, if we don't raise the money, then he'll be forced to re-list the property right after we ring in the new year," he said.

Clara sighed. "Man, talk about laying on the pressure. We'll have the lighting ceremony, the concert, and the boat parade at the end of this week. Your parents will fly in just in time for the festivities. Then the shoppers will have a couple more weeks to enjoy the illuminated streets, visit the shops, and make donations, and then that's it... yikes."

Clara began pacing around. "That's it. We have to maximize our efforts. What we're doing is not nearly enough," she said.

"What else can we do? We have all hands on deck, operating at full capacity. Just look around us."

He pointed toward the helpers propping up a ladder to reach the top of the street lamps, and then toward Mack, who was serving hot chocolate, and even Agnes, who was hanging a wreath.

"I know, and this is wonderful, but what if we ask the business owners if we can place decorated donation buckets with fliers near their cash registers?" she said.

"Okayyy."

She continued to pace. "And... what if we double the amount of volunteers to stand on the street corners ringing their bells and taking up donations?"

"Okay." He repeated.

"And... what if we beg Clay to do a series of mini

concerts until Christmas... you know, over the next couple of weekends? We could say something like come join us every weekend for Christmas Nights with Clay?"

"Sounds good to me, but I'm not so sure Clay would like it. He came home to enjoy spending time with his family, not to work," he said.

"Leave the details up to me. I'll talk to Mack, and I'm sure she can help me figure out a plan to smooth things over with Mrs. Dudley and Clay. I'm almost certain of it."

Mike approached Clara, excitedly grabbing her by the shoulders.

"Have I ever told you how amazing you are?" he asked.

"At least a thousand times." She smiled.

"Good. Well, here's to one-thousand and one. This is a genius idea, and I don't know why I didn't think of it myself. If this doesn't help us bring in the funds for the warehouse and ultimately save Lighthouse Tours, then at least we can say we gave it our best shot." Mike kissed Clara several times, practically smothering her and making her squeal.

Mackenzie walked over holding two cups of hot chocolate in hand, grinning at the two lovebirds.

"Clara, I don't know what you're doing to the guy, but he can't seem to get enough of you." Mack smiled while handing over their beverages.

"Here, I was hoping this would warm you up.

The breeze coming off the water is giving me a chill in my bones." She continued.

They each took a cup, thanking her for the added whipped cream.

"Mackenzie, you are a godsend. Thanks for setting up the hot cocoa station," Mike said.

"It's my pleasure."

"All right... I'm going to leave you two to talk while I check in with Jonathan, Mae, and Tommy. Last I heard, Mae has grand plans for decorating the fleet. I can't wait to see what she's up to." He turned to Clara for one last peck before heading back to the store.

Later that evening, Mack carefully balanced her feet, walking across Brody's back as he laid on his living room floor. According to Brody, he watched a buddy of his use the same technique whenever his back ached. He thought it was a sure-fire way to work out the kinks. Mack wasn't so sure.

"Brody, the entertainment is non-stop when I'm with you. I'm not sure if this method is helping or making your back worse, but it sure does make for an interesting date," she said.

"Inch lower, toward my spine... yep, that's it... knead your feet into that area for a while."

"What in the world did you do to your back? Did

you overdo it while decorating earlier today?" she asked.

"Eight hours of climbing up and down a ladder may have triggered it, or maybe we're going to get some rain. Who knows? My back has never been the same since I got into an accident years ago. It comes along with the territory."

"Oh, Brody. I'm sorry to hear that. Was it a terrible car accident?" she asked.

"It was a classic case of texting while driving. The woman behind me slammed her car into me, causing me to lunge forward into someone else. The car was totaled, but thankfully, I walked away without a scratch. Every once in a while my back likes to remind me about that day, but I'm mostly thankful because it could've been worse."

"I'll bet," she replied.

"The only thing I wish I could change is not having my back give me such a hard time while I'm supposed to be in the middle of a romantic evening with my lady."

"Your lady?" She paused just above his spine, still smiling, but he couldn't tell.

"Did I say something out of line?" he asked.

"No... no... not at all. Truthfully, I like the way it sounds. I like the idea of being your lady." She giggled.

"I'm glad. I really care about you, Mackenzie.

When we're not together, I think about you all the time."

Mackenzie continued kneading her feet into his back while staring down at her red toenail polish. On the inside, she felt excited, but wasn't quite sure what to say. It had been a long time since she felt this way about anyone... not even Bill measured up to his standard.

"Hey, Mack?"

"Yes."

"Can you come down here with me for a moment?"

"Sure."

Brody rolled over, making room for her to lie over a large buck on his rustic area rug. His style was more on the outdoorsy side, with deer antlers decorating the walls, and a faux log which served as his coffee table.

"What's on your mind?" she asked.

He hesitated.

"This may sound a little cheesy, but I think it's important that you know my intentions," he replied.

"Oh, silly. I know you have good intentions. You're a good guy. Everybody knows it, Brody."

"Thanks. But that's not what I meant. I just want you to know that I'm really enjoying our time together... and I have every intention of dating you purposefully. As in... dating you to see if it will lead to something more serious someday. I'm not trying to scare you off by getting too serious too soon. But my intentions toward you and Steph are good. I really care about you guys," he said.

As she listened to him, she continued looking up toward the deer antler chandelier hanging above them while processing every word.

"Brody, that's the sweetest thing anyone has ever said to me. Even sweeter because I know you're sincere," she responded, slipping her hand over his.

"I think you're a real good influence for my girl. You're honest, loyal, gentle, and kind. As long as you always consider her heart along with mine, then I think everything will be good between us. Now... and in the future." She continued.

"You have my word, Mack."

He rolled her over him, tickling her and making her laugh, before settling in with a passionate kiss.

"Ahh, looks like your back is feeling all better." She teased.

"What can I say. It looks like a little one-on-one time with you makes me forget about my troubles."

Mackenzie sat up and looked around his place.

"Speaking of troubles... the lack of Christmas decorations in this cabin of yours is very worrisome. No tree? No garland... no tensile... nothing? With all the decorating you did over at my place and up and down the streets of Solomons Island today, one would think this place would be sparkling with all that glitters and shines. What happened?"

Brody slowly raised himself up, looking around, nodding.

"I'm guilty as charged. I don't know what happened. Somehow I take more pleasure in helping others I guess," he said.

"Oh, yeah. Well, Steph and I have our work cut out for us then. Tonight, when I pick her up from her playdate, we're going to map out a plan that involves sprucing this place up for the holidays. Maybe we can even swing by after we help you get the tree set up at the gazebo tomorrow. That, plus we have to figure out another day to reschedule the bonfire. Man, we're going to be busy."

"Don't worry about it. We'll figure it out. As for the tree, if I'm going to be in any kind of shape to lift another tree, then I need to come up with a plan. I hate to admit it, but I may need to rub some cream on my back, lay on a heating pad tonight, and even wear a brace just to ensure the tree makes it to the gazebo in one piece." He laughed.

"Or we can be wise about this and have a few of the guys pick it up for you. There's no sense in throwing your back out completely, Brody."

"I guess you're right." He paused for a long moment.

"I can think of something that may help keep my back in line," he said, pointing to her lips. "If you plant those sweet lips on me one more time, I think it might be enough to help me get through tomorrow. What do you say?"

"Brody, get over here. Somehow I think that back of yours is going to be just fine."

Mack snuggled with Brody, helping him to forget about everything that ailed him that evening, and feeling hopeful about their future together.

CHAPTER 11

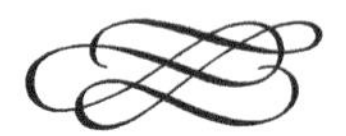

"Mae, since you have no idea what you want for Christmas, I took it upon myself to settle on the perfect gift," Jonathan said, proudly.

"What is it?"

"If I told you, it wouldn't be a surprise," he replied.

They sat at the kitchen counter, enjoying a slow morning as they ate breakfast. In a couple of hours they would prepare for the kickoff to Christmas Nights, but for now, Mae grumbled over scrambled eggs, wondering what he could possibly have up his sleeve.

"Can you give me a hint?"

"Not even the slightest. Nice try, though," he said.

"That's fine. Besides, the only thing I really want for Christmas is a good health report from your doctor. That's it. Anything else is a bonus."

"About that," he replied.

Mae placed her fork down, giving Jonathan her full attention.

"I called the doctor's office again as promised, requesting another test. He was pretty straightforward with me, Mae. He said my test was covered under my annual physical, and it's uncommon for patients to repeat the same bloodwork unless it was for a specific reason."

"It was for a specific reason," she said.

"Maeee."

"All right, I'm listening." She surrendered.

"Thank you… now where was I? Oh, yes. He did explain that my A1c levels were at five point eight. According to him, the pre-diabetic stage ranges anywhere from five point seven to six point four. He recommended I cut back on my sugar, and exercise for thirty minutes per day."

"That's nonsense. Did you eat the morning of your physical? You know they say you're not supposed to eat, Jonathan. It spoils the results every time."

"No, Mae. I didn't eat. I followed the nurse's instructions to a tee," he replied.

"I just don't understand it, to be honest. It's not like we overindulge or anything. Yes, sure, I bake an occasional cake for you. Maybe even a cookie or two from the cookie jar, but that's it. I think he's overreacting," she said, sounding flustered.

Jonathan finished the last of his breakfast before responding.

"I know you're concerned, but we're not doctors. I don't like the idea of being pre-diabetic any more than you do. But the news could be worse. If all I have to do is buy a treadmill, or start taking neighborhood walks, then so be it. I'll even skip out on my usual tradition of eating pie for breakfast on Christmas morning. Whatever it takes, as long as I get to be with my family, I'm not putting up a fuss, and neither should you." He waved the whole thing off, wanting to have nothing more to do with the conversation.

Mae watched Jonathan rinse his plate and stack his dishes in the dishwasher before continuing on.

"You're right. It could be much worse. We're pretty blessed to have each other, and I'm willing to do whatever it takes to support you. If it means changing my eating habits and baking, then so be it. We're in this together." She offered.

A smile returned to Jonathan's face. "Thanks, Mae. Although whatever you do, please don't change the menu during the holidays on my account. The kids look forward to your honey glazed ham and pies. I'll just watch my portions and do a better job with exercising. Hopefully, this way the doctor will be pleased with next year's test results," he said.

"I sure hope so."

Amid their conversation, there was a knocking sound at the front door. Mae looked up front and caught a glimpse of Meredith, the next-door neighbor, peering in through the glass panels alongside their door.

"Jonathan, remind me to stop by the blind store on Monday. The head of the nosey association is peering right into our living room," she said, while flopping around in her slippers as she walked to the front door.

"Good morning, Meredith. You're up nice and early." Mae greeted her with a pleasant smile, even while harboring not so pleasant thoughts.

"Good morning, Mae. I won't keep you long. I just thought you'd be interested in knowing the winners for the decorating contest will be chosen soon. Everyone agreed to wait a couple of days, giving time for the Zimmermans to get on board. Turns out they'll be taking part after all."

"Well, isn't that wonderful?"

"Yes... yes. After all, we're an all-inclusive neighborhood." She smiled, trying her best to look around the house while talking to Mae.

"Is there anything else I can help you with?"

"No. I suppose I'll see you and Jonathan this

evening at the tree lighting ceremony?" Meredith asked.

"Of course, Jonathan and I will be running the boat parade. We plan on passing by the gazebo area right before Clay starts his concert. The decorated boats will be gorgeous. You don't want to miss it."

"Oh... so you're a part of the festivities. I had no idea," she said, appearing to be shocked.

"I thought surely the mayor's office would've called and informed you personally. What a shame!" Mae teased.

As soon as Meredith caught on to Mae's sarcasm, she held her chin up and wished her a good day before returning to her side of the yard.

"Hi, Fran. This is Clara Covington. We met the night I ran out of gas. You and your husband were gracious to let me wait at your store for my ride to arrive. Remember me?"

"Yes, how could I forget you, dear?" Fran said, on the other end of the line.

"How are you?"

"I'm doing well. My husband and I were just talking about you the other day. We were wondering how things were going with you and your sister," Fran asked.

"Things are going surprisingly well. She's busy

working all the time, but it's nice having her here on the island."

"I'll bet. Glad to hear that all is well," she said.

"I sincerely meant to call you long before now... and I realize this is very last minute. But I was wondering if you and Jeffrey would like to join us for our tree lighting ceremony and the kickoff to Christmas Nights this evening? I don't know if you recall, but my fiancé owns a boating company, and we're putting on a boat parade. There will also be a benefit concert featuring one of our local country singers."

"Christmas Nights...yes... I know all about it. We've been coming down to visit for years. To this day, I haven't seen anything like it. We were just talking about how behind we are with our Christmas shopping, so I can't think of a better place to be."

"Perfect. You're more than welcome to join us on the boat parade if you'd like. Well, to be honest by 'us' I really mean some of our teammates from Lighthouse Tours. If I even think about stepping one foot on a moving boat, my motion sickness kicks right in," Clara replied.

"Honey, how in the world did you get a job working at a boating company with motion sickness?" She chuckled.

"It's a long story... I'll have to share those details over coffee someday."

"I look forward to hearing it. In the meantime,

we'll see you this evening. Maybe we can even bring Amelia, our granddaughter."

"That's a wonderful idea."

"Sounds good. I'll see you later."

"Take care."

Clara hung up, noticing a picture of her and Mike sitting beside the phone on her desk. It was taken the evening they got engaged, standing by the horses on the beach. It was the same night she committed to being by his side through the best and most challenging times.

She hoped this Christmas would prove to be one of the better times, bringing about a fresh start for the business, beginning this evening with Christmas Nights

"Oh... my... goodness. This is so amazing, Mike. We did it. We really pulled it off," Clara said, excitedly taking in the size of the crowd gathered for the ceremony.

"Would you look at the turnout? I have a really good feeling about this." She continued.

"It is a nice turnout, but let's not get too far ahead of ourselves. This is only the beginning."

"I know, but still. We have to stay positive. Now... according to my watch, it's a couple of minutes before the hour. Why don't you head up to the gazebo with

Mayor Thompson, and I'm going to camp out with Agnes and Mack, and then head over to the fleet to make sure the crew is okay."

"You sure you don't want to come on stage with us? I didn't organize this whole thing on my own. You played a major role, Clara," he said, reaching his hand out to her.

"That's so sweet. Thank you for the recognition, but you know I operate best behind the scenes, love. You can go up and represent the both of us. I'll make sure I capture a few pictures to hang at the office."

"Okay." Mike leaned in for a good luck kiss and made his way to the front of the crowd to join Mayor Thompson.

In the meantime, Clara searched the crowd, spotting Agnes, Mack, and a few others from the café.

"Okay, ladies. This is it. The moment we've been waiting for," Clara said.

"Oh, Clara, I've been a nervous wreck all morning. First, I was worried about Brody going overboard with his back while lifting the tree this morning. Now, I'm nervous about the lights. Did you hear the news? We had at least three sets of new lightbulbs blow out on us this morning during the test run. I literally thought I was going to break out into a cold sweat." Mack complained.

"Brody didn't mention it."

"Of course, he wouldn't. You know how men are." Mack sighed.

Agnes leaned in to reassure her. "Don't worry, Mackenzie, I'm sure everything will be smooth sailing now that he's worked out the kinks. I have to say, I don't think I've ever experienced anything like this. Christmas festivities were completely different in New York where Clara and I grew up," she said.

Clara laughed. "That's an understatement. We were surrounded by the hustle and bustle of a big city. Picture this... dirty snow piled up at every street corner and tall buildings everywhere. It was literally a concrete jungle," she said.

"I can't imagine anything like that. I've lived on the island for so long, anything else would be very foreign to me," Mack replied.

"Clara, I'll admit, although city life was very different, there was still something magical about it. We had a lot of fond memories of the holidays. Remember how mom and dad used to take us down to Rockefeller Center every year to go ice skating?" Agnes asked.

"Oh, yeah. How could I forget? We used to skate until our toes and fingertips were numb.... and that was with our gloves on. Then there was our pretzel tradition. We couldn't afford to dine at the fancy restaurant on the rink, but Dad always made sure we had hot chocolate and pretzels from one of the nearby vendors." She smiled, recalling the memory like it was yesterday.

"Yep, and it was tradition for us to head down the

street to St. Patrick's Cathedral afterward and light a candle in the chapel. It seemed like there were always crowds of people piling in to do the same. I don't know about you, but back then, Christmas wasn't the same without those traditions," Agnes said.

"You're right, Ag. It was a special time. Just talking about it makes me miss mom and dad even more."

Mackenzie stood before the ladies, holding them both by the hand.

"This is what the spirit of Christmas is really all about. Just listening to the two of you bonding over special childhood memories warms my heart. It doesn't matter where you are, whether it be back in the city, or here on the island. As long as you have love surrounding you, that's all that matters. I love you guys," she said, squeezing their hands.

"I have two words for you, Mackenzie. Tear... jerker. You're going to make me cry." Agnes chuckled.

"Aww, well it's true. Ever since Clara moved here, she's been like a sister to me, which makes you my sister, too," Mack replied.

"Okay, you two. Group hug and let's pull it together. It looks like Mike and Mayor Thompson are hitting the stage."

The ladies came together quickly and returned to giving their full attention toward the gazebo.

"Good evening, ladies and gentlemen." Mayor Thompson announced.

"It brings me great pleasure to announce to you our tenth annual tree lighting and kickoff to Christmas Nights."

The crowd cheered. Clara anxiously awaited the big moment while noticing Brody in ready position near the tree, and Jonathan signaling with a thumbs up, much further down the dock by the boats.

The mayor continued his speech.

"I would be remiss if I didn't first acknowledge the special highlights of this year's ceremony and how it all came to be. As many of you read on our fliers and publications, this year is like no other. For a brief moment we came very close to not having Christmas Nights due to an issue with our former contractors. Thankfully, the team over at Lighthouse Tours stepped in, enlisting the help of others, and making this year's event possible. It's because of Lighthouse Tours that you will enjoy this phenomenal tree lighting, a Christmas walk down the illuminated Main Street as you shop, a boat parade, which will begin momentarily, and our very own Clay Nathan, as he sings a few Christmas selections for tonight's concert. So, for that, let's give a hand to Mike Sanders, of Lighthouse Tours, and Clara Covington, standing in the crowd."

Again, the crowd erupted in cheers with joyful

anticipation. Mike and Clara both waved and smiled to those around them.

"Before I hand this over to Mike, I'd like to highlight the benefit portion of this gathering today. It has come to my attention that many of the residents of Solomons Island are seeking a place for commercial boat storage. We have a unique opportunity that would benefit us as residents and Lighthouse Tours. With that in mind, I will now turn this over to Mike so he can explain."

The crowd continued offering a supportive cheer as he approached the microphone.

"Good evening, good folks of Solomons Island. This won't take long as I know many of you are excited to get down to the main attraction." He pointed toward the tree.

"Tonight, we thought it was important that you know, Lighthouse Tours is working hard to provide you a full-service boat storage facility, but in order to do so, we need your help in purchasing the warehouse, currently owned by Dylan McPherson, of McPherson and Sons. He's generously taken the warehouse off the market, temporarily giving us time to raise the necessary funds and to weed out unwanted competition. I'm sure most of you may be wondering how this would benefit Solomons Island. So, here's what we would be willing to offer. We would elicit local help to get the warehouse up and running by next summer, completely paying for all renovations. We would also be able to provide shrink wrap and storage options for those who want it. The funds earned by the facility would go to employees' salaries, maintenance, a small percentage for reinvestment of the business, and we would offer a continued promise to provide low-cost storage for residents only."

The crowd erupted.

"Hold on… there's more. A percentage will be set aside each year to fund Christmas Nights. This would be written in an agreement so we never have to worry about poor quality service from contractors again."

It was hard for Mike to contain the crowd as they continued to express their approval. When the noise simmered down, he continued.

"Finally, we all know how much the tourists enjoy our Christmas walk as they shop… so let's give a hand to those who are visiting. Without them, where would we be?"

Clara leaned in and whispered to the girls.

"Wow, Mike is really working the crowd and they absolutely love him," she said.

"Did you expect anything less?" Mack smiled.

Mike continued.

"In order to make this happen we need your support. Our volunteers will be lined along Main Street and in stores taking up donations. If you support the idea of having the boat storage run by Lighthouse

Tours, then please be sure to stop by one of our stands and make a donation. We're accepting cash and checks and will be collecting all the way up to the last day of December. Now.... without further ado... are you ready for the best tree lighting, boat tour, concert, and Christmas shopping experience you've ever had?" He roared.

The crowd roared back and joined Mike in the official countdown. Brody was on standby near the cords, and when the tree lit up, with the star shining so bright, Clara swore she caught a glimpse of a shooting star in the backdrop.

By the end of the evening, Clara's guests disembarked the boat led by Jonathan and Mae. In the background, the speakers on the dock bellowed Christmas music and a few stragglers remained, admiring the lights on the fleet.

"Clara, we can't thank you enough for inviting us to come out and enjoy the parade. Jeffrey and Amelia enjoyed themselves immensely, didn't you, dear?" Fran said.

"We had a delightful time. Jonathan and Mae can give me a tour of the island anytime." Jeffrey chuckled.

"It was a pleasure having you. I'm sorry you didn't get a chance to walk down Main Street and shop. Perhaps you can return for another visit before Christmas?" Clara asked.

"Oh, you bet. Amelia here has been saving her money, and we certainly need to check off a few items on our list," Fran replied.

Jonathan approached Jeffrey, patting him on the back. They became fast friends on the boat ride, realizing they had quite a bit in common.

"Jeffrey, anytime you and the Mrs. want to join us, all you have to do is say the word. You have my number. Don't be a stranger. This spring we'll be setting sail in our new boat, and we'd love to have you. Maybe you could even join us for dinner," he said.

"It sounds like a plan, my friend."

Mike joined the group, thanking everyone for their participation.

"Hey, everybody. This night wouldn't have been a success without you. Thank you to everyone for coming out to show your support," he said.

"Mike, have you heard any feedback about the first night of donations? I wonder how much we've collected so far," Jonathan asked.

"No, not yet. We'll have a tally by the morning. A part of me is too nervous to find out," Mike responded.

Mack and Brody poked their heads in just in time to hear what was going on.

"Not sure why you would be nervous. I'm sure I'm not the only one who witnessed the massive crowd who showed up to hear Clay Nathan. People showed up in droves and were shoving cash and checks in the donation baskets to the point where some volunteers were having difficulty keeping up," Mack said.

"See, I told you there was nothing to worry about. Solomons has your back," Clara said, poking Mike in the belly.

"I know... I know... but you never can be too sure about these things. We have a mighty steep hill to climb in order to put a down payment on the warehouse. We need a lot of cheddar to get the ball rolling in the right direction... to the tune of twenty thousand dollars... and don't forget... if we don't raise it, then the warehouse goes back on the market and good ole Logan Woods moves right on in, ready to stake his claim and our business," Mike said.

"Man, twenty thousand is nothing. These pop stars make that in the blink of an eye at their concerts...and in this case, Clay isn't charging anything, and he's performing every weekend up until Christmas. It doesn't get any sweeter than this." Brody added.

Jan from the North Beach office also tried to reassure him. She was one of the volunteers ringing bells for donations on Main Street.

"They filled my bucket to the brim every hour like clockwork. I don't see how this couldn't be a success. Especially with the tourists turning out this year. There's no way that crowd was filled with people just from Solomons Island," she said.

Fran took a step closer to Mike. She graciously thanked him for hosting the event and then left him with a few parting words.

"Mike, we don't know each other very well, but I'm going to give you the same advice I gave your sweet Clara when she spent time at our store. Just hang in there and have faith. It will all work out. You're doing great things for this island. It's evident in all the conversations I overheard this evening. Whatever you do, don't give up. See it through until the end," Fran said.

She gave him and Clara a hug, made promises to come and visit again soon, and bid them a good night.

The group scattered in different directions, preparing to head home for the evening. Mike and Clara lingered on the dock, talking about the day's events.

"Mike... I have two words for you," she said.

"I'm all ears."

"Crackling fireplace," Clara responded.

"Come again?"

"There's nothing like a cozy fireplace with a view of the beach to help you relax. This evening was amazing, but I'm exhausted, and all I want to do is kick my feet up by the fire and listen to the sound of the water. What do you say?"

"It does sound nice."

"Great. We can debrief about everything over a

glass of wine. Agnes headed back early to get ready for work, so it will be a quiet evening for two," she said in a melodious voice.

"You don't have to twist my arm. I'll follow you in the jeep." He slid his hand beside her waist, leaning in and inhaling the aroma of her hair.

Clara wondered if it was normal for two people to have such an insane level of attraction for one another. But, regardless of whether it was, she loved it, and hoped it would last a lifetime.

"Mae, do you remember the Christmas gift I mentioned the other day?" Jonathan asked.

"The one you said was a secret? I remember. I don't understand why you would bring it up if you have no intention of telling me what it is." She grumbled.

They gathered their belongings and walked slowly toward their car, admiring all the Christmas lights down Main Street.

"I didn't tell you because I didn't think it would be fair," he replied.

"Fair? Jonathan, what are you talking about? We're not little children. I don't have to wait until the clock strikes twelve on Christmas in order to open my gifts." She continued to fuss.

"Uh huh. That's not quite what I meant. I don't

think it would be fair to those who worked so hard to surprise you."

Mae stopped in her tracks with an irritated on her face. She was oblivious to her surroundings and wondered why Jonathan was speaking in some sort of Morse code.

"Just come out and say what's on your mind, Jonathan. If I didn't know any better, I'd think this cool evening breeze is having an effect on you." She fussed.

Jonathan turned and held Mae by the shoulders.

"Sweetheart, I didn't think it would be fair to your family who worked so hard to surprise you. A few people who you love dearly are here to see you this evening. Turn around and look across the street."

Mae turned around in slow motion, appearing to be in complete disbelief at what she saw. It was her daughter Lily, her son-in-law, Steven, and her two grandkids who she hadn't seen in a very long time.

"Oh, my. Is that who I think it is?" She squealed, walking across the street to greet her family.

"Is that my baby and my grand-babies ... and my son-in-law standing right before my very eyes?" she said, laughing and tearing up at the same time.

"It sure is. Surprise, grandma. We're happy to see you," Shelby replied, running toward Mae.

Her granddaughter and her brother hugged her first and then made room for their parents.

"Hi, Mom. I just want to go on record and tell

you I love you... I miss you... and Jonathan is totally to blame for us being here a week earlier than originally planned." Lily teased, squeezing her mother tight, and winking at Jonathan after telling on him.

Steven came forward and greeted Mae as well. Although it had been a while, they were all close and fell right in sync, as if they'd seen each other the day prior.

"Mom, I know what you're going to say... it's been too long since I last brought your grand-babies here to see you. I come bearing peace offerings hoping you can forgive me." Steven teased.

"Oh, come here, you. Give me a hug," Mae said.

"I'm just so sorry that everyone missed the boat parade and the tree lighting ceremony. How long have you been waiting out here in the street?" she asked.

"Mom, we didn't miss a thing. We saw you and Jonathan leading the parade, we caught Mike giving his speech to the crowd, and we even fit in a little shopping, didn't we, babe?" Lily said.

"Yep."

Jonathan proudly towed Shelby's little brother around in his arms while waiting for everyone to get reacquainted.

"We were tempted to hop on the boat with you but didn't want to distract you from doing your job." Lily confessed.

"Oh, you wouldn't have been a distraction. I'm

just happy to have you here. What about school? Don't the kids have class for a few more days before they let out for Christmas break?" Mae asked.

Lily pointed toward Jonathan.

"I told you she was going to ask questions. This one is on you, Jonathan. Maybe you can explain to mom why we're here early."

Jonathan put Lily's son down and took his wife by the hand.

"I know how much you missed the family, dear. When Lily and I got to talking about it, we thought it might be nice to have a little extra time together, that's all. I went ahead and fixed up the sheets in the guests' rooms, and Steven and I are going to do all the cooking. All you have to do is sit back and enjoy the family," Jonathan said.

"You and Steven are going to do what?" Mae asked.

Everyone burst into laughter at the thought. They all knew full well that Jonathan couldn't cook to save his life. And if he did make something, it was nothing they'd want to eat.

CHAPTER 12

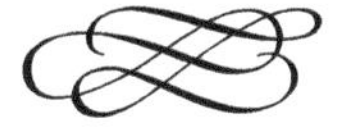

At the café, Mackenzie was joined by Mrs. Dudley and Clara, talking over a slice of pie about their plans for the rest of Christmas Nights.

"Mrs. Dudley, thank you so much for talking Clay into putting on the benefit concert for us. We feel so lucky to have him. We know how much of a sacrifice he's making to do this during his time off," Mackenzie said, taking in her next bite of pie.

"Clay was happy to do it. I could barely get the words out of my mouth before he was picking up his guitar to practice a few Christmas songs. He would do anything to please his grandmother. Perhaps this will also help to smooth things over between myself and Chef Harold," Mrs. Dudley said, peering over her mug.

Mack raised her eyebrow at Clara and then redirected her attention toward Mrs. Dudley.

"What do you mean? Things are fine with you and Chef Harold," Mack said.

"Oh, come on, Mackenzie. You can be straightforward with me. I've heard the chatter about me being the grumpy old woman who orders the Monday special on the wrong day of the week. You don't have to pretend." She explained.

Mack shrunk in her seat a bit and stopped eating her pie. "You know about that?" she said in a low voice.

"Word gets around... either that or I have really great hearing. It's no big deal. The truth is, I owe you guys an apology," Mrs. Dudley said.

"What! Oh for goodness' sake, you don't owe us anything. You've been a regular here at the café for quite some time, and if it wasn't for regulars like yourself, we wouldn't be in business." Mack argued.

"Thank you, Mackenzie. But, I still want to say I'm sorry. I've been everything folks have described and more. Grumpy, old, miserable, lonely, sitting all by myself in the corner of the café... I'm sure I could go on. It's a wonder you continue to speak to me. Then again, I guess you had no choice since it's your job to serve."

"Mrs. Dudley, take it from me when I tell you that Mack loves having you here. She's expressed her appreciation and called you by name... scout's honor," Clara said, vouching for her friend.

"I believe it. I just thought it was time I take ownership of my behavior. I wasn't always this way, you know. There was a time when I was a lot more outgoing and friendly... until my daughter passed away two years ago. She was a grown woman, but forever my baby girl. I watched her slip away right before my very eyes. An aggressive form of cancer suddenly snatched her life away... leaving two girls behind. The Monday night special was her absolute favorite meal in the world. She used to ask me to make it for her every time she came to visit." Mrs. Dudley's voice trailed off.

The ladies were caught off guard, feeling stunned by the news. To Mack, the special they served was taking on a whole new meaning.

"Just so you know... it's always my intention to come here on Mondays and order the special on the right day of the week. But, it's the hardest day for me to get out of bed. Lacey passed away on a Monday, and you'd think almost two years later I'd be over it by now, but I'm not. It's the one day of the week I prefer to keep the shades drawn and forget about everything. Including the day she died." She explained.

"Mrs. Dudley, I'm so sorry. Words cannot express how heavy my heart is. To know you've been suffering through this on your own. Why haven't you ever said anything before now? I never realized you went through something so tragic," Mack replied.

"Everybody has their way of dealing with pain. For me... well... I didn't want the attention that comes along with sharing. Grieving was hard enough. Even now, my intent is not to gain sympathy from anybody. I'm taking it one day at a time. It may take the rest of my life to heal, and if it does, that's okay. In the meantime, I just wanted you to know that when you reached out to me about Clay, it made me feel needed again. No matter how small my role was, it gave me something to do... and something to look forward to this Christmas season. So... sincerely... thank you, Mackenzie. Not only to you, but to Chef Harold for putting up with me."

"Aww, Mrs. Dudley, can I give you a hug? I could cry right now."

Mackenzie reached across the table, squeezing Mrs. Dudley as hard as she could.

"Oh, dear." Mrs. Dudley chuckled.

Mackenzie continued. "You don't know how much this fills my heart. It may sound silly, but I view you guys as my family... my café family. I care about every one of you. I could share stories for days about how this place helped put food on my table, especially while I was struggling to raise my daughter on my own," she said.

"Okay, seriously. There must be something in the air this week. This is the second time my eyes have welled into tears, and both times I was with you, Mackenzie." Clara teased.

Mrs. Dudley wore a big smile on her face. "Crying is good medicine for the soul. Let it out, girl. Let it out." She encouraged.

Mack listened to Mrs. Dudley share some more stories of how the Monday night special came to be her favorite. She took it all in... occasionally looking around, feeling thankful for the big and the little things. Thankful for the bridge club, arguing over who cheated during the last round, thankful for Josh, and Dakota... and even thankful that she lived among such wonderful people who would band together when someone was in need.

"Mackenzie, are you still with us?" Clara asked.

"Yes, I'm here. Just hearing Mrs. Dudley's story, and talking to the both of you, reminds me I have a lot to be grateful for, that's all," Mack said.

Mrs. Dudley chimed in. "Yes, we all do. But enough about me. There's something I've been meaning to share with you, Clara."

"Me?"

"Yes, it's about your sister, Agnes. I'm not sure if either of you have noticed, but it appears as though she has an admirer," she said.

"I hadn't noticed. I don't think she has either. Who is it?" Clara asked.

"Do you swear to secrecy?" Mrs. Dudley said.

"Yes, ma'am. Although you have me very curious at this point."

"It's the new guy in town. I think he's an author... or at least that's what I overheard when questioned by the lady at the front desk at the library. I've seen him over there a time or two, clicking away on his laptop. He's good-looking if you ask me, and clearly he thinks the same about Agnes, as he couldn't seem to get enough of her at the ceremony yesterday," she replied.

Mack soaked up every word. "Stop it. Agnes hasn't been here that long, and she already has a secret crush? We have to find out who this guy is. I hope he stops by the café soon so we can get the scoop on him." She chuckled.

"Well, I don't want to be a Debbie downer, but Agnes' head is so far buried in the sand between the Seafood Shack and her trying to get the food truck started this summer, I highly doubt she has time to entertain an admirer. Plus, she said she's taking off a year from dating. So far she appears to be sticking to it." Clara confessed.

"Booo. Taking a year off for what? You can't help who you meet and fall in love with. Just look at you and Mike. One day you go flying out of here on a mission to find a job... and bam... you reverse your car into his... and the next thing you know you've been struck by cupid's arrow." Mack teased.

"Mack, I love you dearly, but you are such a nut." Clara laughed.

"Call me what you want, but you know I'm telling the truth."

The ladies returned to their planning, discussing details for Clay's upcoming show, and the latest gossip about the new author in town.

"Flowers for the lady," Mike said, presenting Clara with a bouquet as he cradled her gently from behind.

"Mike, you startled me. Did Agnes let you in?" she asked.

"She did, and she told me I could find you upstairs wrapping gifts. I hope you don't mind me coming up to surprise you."

"Not at all," Clara said, closing her eyes, taking in all the love and attention he had to offer.

"Honestly, I needed a break. Doing the extra work for Christmas Nights has been fun, but I'm exhausted these days. A romantic break is always welcomed by you," she said.

Mike spun her around and laid the bouquet down on her dresser.

"I'm sorry, I've been so laser focused on everything that's going on that I've neglected to take care of you. None of this is more important than us. You do know that, right?"

"Of course, I do, silly. I know this busy time won't last forever," she replied, resting her head on his shoulders.

"Speaking of Christmas Nights, where are the numbers as of today?" Clara asked.

"Last time I checked, we're at fifty-five hundred. It's a good start, but we definitely have a way to go."

"Well, we just have to hunker down, continue to work hard, and remember Fran's advice about having faith." She encouraged.

"That's all we can do. In the meantime... is that what I think it is?" he asked, pointing toward her bed.

Clara had a variety of gifts covering the bed, ranging from a back massage, to a dream machine, a night robe, and more.

"It depends on what you think it is." She giggled.

"The dream machine is what dad wants for Christmas. How did you find this thing? I've been searching all over town with no such luck."

"I had a few tricks up my sleeve. It's not about where to go. It's all about who you know."

"Oh, excuse me. Well, please, thank your connection for me. Dad is going to be thrilled when he sees this."

After inspecting the gift, he nestled closer to her again.

"Hey, Clara."

"Yes, my love."

"Thank you for everything you're doing to make

things special for my parents when they arrive. It means a lot to me that all of you are finally coming together to meet. I'm so happy about it I feel like I could walk down the aisle with you this month, tossing everything to the wind, and just making you my own," he said.

"Mike Sanders, you wouldn't dare do that to the women in your family."

"Why not? What's wrong with it? I kind of like the idea, actually. We could bypass the planning, skip straight to the honeymoon, and move in at the beginning of the new year. Jonathan and Mae did it and everything worked out just fine," he said.

"Yeah, but I'll bet it disappointed her family that they couldn't be a part of their ceremony."

"Clara... my love... unlike Jonathan and Mae... you'll have your sister, Agnes, and I'll have my parents. It's not like we come from large families."

"Mike... my love... I want a proper wedding. My parents were traditional and so am I. But, if it will make you happy, we can consider moving the wedding up from next summer to perhaps early spring?"

"Okay," Mike said, sounding a little melancholy, but still supportive.

He playfully ran his fingers through her hair.

"You can't blame a guy for trying. I just want our lives as Mr. and Mrs. Sanders to begin as soon as possible, that's all," he said.

"I know, babe, and I want the same thing. The

good news is I don't even want a complicated wedding. Just something simple, yet elegant. Maybe a sweet ceremony by the cliffs overlooking the beach and the water. Or maybe even in a ceremony in Chesapeake where we got engaged. Whatever the final plans are, just hang in there a little while longer. I promise you it will be worth the wait."

"You know I will. I want whatever makes you happy."

"Thank you." She gave him a quick peck and put him to work.

"Now, I'll need your help to get the wrapped gifts downstairs and placed under the tree. This house needs to be absolutely perfect when your parents come over to visit. What time are they arriving again?" she asked.

"Friday around noon."

"Perfect. We can take them to dinner on Friday night, and on Saturday they can come to Clay's concert and perhaps enjoy a little shopping." She smiled.

"That's the plan."

"Excellent... and when you bring them over, I'll have plenty of hors d'oeuvres and snacks, just in case. I was thinking on Sunday we can enjoy a nice family meal after we wrap up with-"

"Clara." Mike called out.

She was so caught up in her plans and thoughts, audibly running through her mental checklist, she hardly heard a thing Mike said. She continued.

"After we wrap up with volunteering, they might want to relax. Oh, and what am I going to wear? I really need to stop it, I'm being ridiculous. I'll be myself, and wear something appropriate for the occasion-"

Mike laughed hard enough to grab her attention.

"What?" she asked.

"You know it's bad when you talk to yourself and then respond to your own questions. I'll say it one more time. You're going to be great, and my parents will absolutely adore you. They already do. Now, put these flowers in water while I take the gifts downstairs."

"But—"

"Clara, no buts." He stuffed his arms with as many gifts as possible and began backing out of her room.

"Just remember what I said. They already think you're amazing. You got this."

She dropped her hands to her side, smiling at his words of encouragement.

"This was nice, Brody. Whisking me away for a spontaneous lunch date for two was an unexpected yet welcomed surprise," Mack said.

"Thanks. I was hoping you'd like the idea. It's healthy to have a change of scenery for lunch every once in a while. Even if it means just hanging out in my truck." He laughed.

"Hey, it's the privacy and the peace and quiet for me. You really are a thoughtful man. Plus, you make one mean croissant sandwich, putting Chef Harold's turkey sandwiches to shame. Of course, you can't tell him I said so. I think it's the mixture of honey mustard and mayo that gets me every time," she said, while savoring the taste of her last bite.

Brody passed her one of her favorite Italian sodas to wash the sandwich down before resting back in the driver's seat.

"Mackenzie."

"Yes?"

He waited in silence for what felt like an eternity, staring outside the window.

"What's the matter, Brody? You were just talking to me and now you look like you've seen a ghost if there was such a thing." She chuckled.

He started to say something and then corrected himself.

"Don't pay me any mind. I guess I'm just having one of my off days. I have so many thoughts swirling around in my head. Sometimes I don't even know where to begin," he said.

"Talk to me. Is something bothering you?" she asked.

"No. In fact, it's quite the opposite."

Mackenzie looked down toward the front seat of

Brody's pickup truck, noticing him nervously tapping his fingers on the steering wheel. She reached out, gliding her hand over his, and waited patiently for him to respond.

"I'm in love with you, Mack. Knee deep, head over heels, whatever you want to call it... that's me in a nutshell. I can't stop thinking about you, and when I'm not with you, all I want to do is see you again. It's like our time together can't come soon enough when we're apart. I hesitated with whether I should say anything. I didn't want to scare you off."

"Oh, sweet Jesus," she whispered.

"I'm sure I know what you're thinking. It's probably over the top, right? We've only been dating for a few months... and I probably need to pump the brakes a little. I get it. I guess I'm just one of those guys who's all in or nothing at—"

"Brody, hold on a minute. I meant nothing bad by it. You just took my breath away, that's all," she replied, giving his hand a little squeeze.

"In a good way?"

"Well, what I'm feeling inside certainly isn't bad. Let's put it this way. It's probably a good thing we're in public." She sniggled.

Brody loosened up a bit, relaxing at her lighthearted reply.

"Okay, this is good. I can handle this kind of response. As long as what I just said doesn't make you want to haul off and knock me out, we're doing good." He laughed.

"Oh, Brody, the thought never crossed my mind. The way you show your love toward me and Steph is so beautiful. Why would I ever want to do anything to mess that up?"

"You wouldn't be the one messing anything up. I was afraid that if I told you explicitly, how I feel — maybe I might come on too strong," he said.

"Never. Everything you said to me is perfect in every way because it's genuine and from the heart. It's been a long time since I had someone speak those words to me. To be honest, the last time someone did, it turns out he wasn't so sincere after all. So, this is a little new for me... but it doesn't mean it's not a good thing."

Brody cupped her hands in the middle of his. "Not that you're asking me, but I still want you to know... I will never be that guy. I will never be the guy of empty promises. Not now... not ever. Your heart is precious to me and I'm going to treat you how you deserve to be treated," he said.

"I know you will, Brody. That's why I can genuinely say that I'm falling for you, too."

Brody drew her in, giving her the most passionate kiss she'd ever experienced from a man. She felt like the stars were aligning in her favor and everything good in her life was about to be even better.

"Oh, dear. Brody, if we don't stop now, I'm going

to be late getting back to the café. I'm supposed to relieve Dakota for lunch."

He took a deep breath, rearranging his collar and his clothing.

"I guess I got a little carried away. These days you have that kind of effect on me."

Mackenzie dove in for one more kiss, not wanting it to end, but knowing it was the right thing to do.

"Come on. We'll pick up where we left off later on. For now, the least I can do is walk you back to the café." He offered.

They begrudgingly got out of the truck and walked hand in hand, returning to the café, happy and in love.

As Mack entered the café, Dakota nearly smacked into her, out of breath, with an urgent look about her. "Mackenzie, don't look now, but the owner's brother-in-law is here. He's waiting at the front counter. He's been here for half an hour, but I didn't have a way to contact you," Dakota said.

Joshua gave her a nod from behind the counter, encouraging her to hurry along.

McKenzie looked back at Brody, suddenly feeling nervous. It was the worst knowing that the boss' brother had been waiting for her, but she tried to keep her composure.

"Would you like for me to hang out for a while?" Brody asked.

"It's okay. Of all the days for me to be late returning from lunch. I feel like a complete idiot. I'll just apologize profusely and then see what he has to say," Mack said.

Dakota and Brody disappeared, giving Mack the space she needed.

She approached the gentleman wearing a suit, extending her hand as he buried his face in a newspaper.

"Good afternoon. It's been a while," she said.

He folded the paper, revealing the profile of a man with a white beard and mustache wearing a flat tweed cap, and a very serious expression on his face.

"Miss Mackenzie. It's nice to see you finally showed up," he said, getting right down to it.

"I'm sorry, sir, I'm not usually late. Today was a special occasion, and it threw me off a little. I really apologize. Can I offer you a refill on your coffee?" she asked.

He relaxed, reaching out his hand to shake hers.

"Please call me by my first name, Edmond. Sir is unnecessary... and I'm good on the refill. Perhaps there's a booth we can grab so we can sit and talk for a while?"

"Sure, right this way, Edmond. We can sit near the window with the best view in the house. It's the perfect angle to glimpse the Christmas tree down at the Gazebo. Have you had a chance to visit?" she asked.

"I have. Apparently Solomons has a lot going on this time of year. I read something about a benefit concert and lots of Christmas shopping. My wife would absolutely love it here."

"I'm sure she would. You should bring her back for the show this weekend," Mack said.

"If only I had time. I have a lot of meetings lined up between now and the week of Christmas. Then the family and I will host everyone at our house this year. Therefore, time is of the essence. On another note, while I was waiting for you, I took a few moments to make some observations about the café."

"I hope you found everything to be in order the way Mr. Garrison likes it. I try my best to run a tight ship around here, making the guests feel welcomed and always ensuring that we go above and beyond with customer service," Mack replied, while tapping her fingers on the table.

"McKenzie, allow me to put your mind at ease. I think you'll find that my visit today will prove to be a positive one. I have nothing but good things to say, and I don't want you to feel you're under any pressure."

She let out a sigh of relief.

"Oh, thank God. I'll admit that your surprise visit made me a little nervous. But, before you go any further, may I ask how Mr. Garrison is doing? I know he mentioned something about being rather ill," she said.

"Unfortunately, I can't say that his health has improved. It's part of the reason I'm here today. Although he was never really the face of The Corner Café, when he bought the place, it was always his intention to make sure the people of Solomons had a second place to call home. Especially whenever they wanted to dine. You've done a phenomenal job at creating a cozy atmosphere where people can eat, indulge in their hobbies, form clubs, and chat over the events of the day. That was his primary goal when he took over from the previous owner. He even hoped to be more involved someday by purchasing a home by the water and establishing roots here. Unfortunately, with his health taking such a turn, he's not certain it will be possible."

"Oh my. I'm so sorry to hear that," she said.

"Mm, trust me. Old Garrison isn't looking for pity. He's as tough as iron... a stubborn fighter ... and he plans on giving his diagnosis a pink slip, sending it right back where it came from. Thankfully, it's not a terminal illness, but it will require a change in lifestyle. Something he's not yet willing to accept. He's rather private by the way, but I'm sure when he comes around to accepting his illness, he'll be more open to sharing what it is."

"Of course, I understand. If I had to deal with such a major life change, I wouldn't want to go broadcasting it either. At least not until I understood the process better and figured a few things out. Just let him know that we're here for him should he ever need his family here at the café." She offered.

"I certainly will."

Mackenzie tried searching her heart for the right way to ask what was on her mind. Things were looking up since Mr. Garrison purchased the café. The moment the for sale sign was taken down, she felt secure in her job, and had even received a promotion to head manager. Now, she wondered if all that progress was about to become a thing of the past.

"Edmond, please take this question the right way... but if Mr. Garrison is ill, what does this mean for the future of the café? It wasn't long ago that we found ourselves in the same position, wondering what we would all do if the place closed indefinitely."

"I'm glad you asked. This brings me to the reason for my visit. I'll be assisting in the process of bringing his ownership to closure."

"Oh," Mackenzie said in a somewhat somber tone.

"However, closure doesn't have to mean selling the café, or closing down for good."

"Oh?" Mack's voice spiked.

Edmond chuckled before proceeding. "My brother would like to offer you an opportunity to become the next owner of the café. He says you deserve it... and honestly, from what I can tell, I have to agree with him."

"Me? An owner? Oh, no. In my dreams, maybe. But, in reality? No way," she responded.

"Why not? You're real savvy with the admin side of things, the finances, and the customers love you. When my brother bought the place, the previous owner said you ran the café like it was your very own. I don't see what the hesitation would be."

"Sadly, it all ties back to one thing," she said, looking around and briefly smiling at the women from the bridge club. Each of them was settled into their card game, wearing the ugliest Christmas sweaters Mack had ever seen.

"And, what's that?" he asked.

"Money. I can't afford to buy this place. No way... no how. I have a little girl to think about. Whatever extra funds I have set aside are for her future."

Edmond nodded.

"What if Garrison offered you a non-traditional opportunity? More specifically... what if we drew up an agreement for a lease-to-own contract? Would that pique your interest?" he asked.

"I'm not sure that I follow... I mean... I know what lease to own is... but I thought people only do that sort of thing for residential sales. Even then, it's rare that you hear of those kinds of deals anymore."

"Rare, but possible. That's exactly what it would be, by the way. A traditional lease-to-own contract, stipulating monthly payments that are affordable and agreeable to you. We could even have a realtor or a lawyer review the paperwork, just so you can rest easy, knowing there's no funny business going on behind the scenes," he responded.

Mack rested flush against the leather seating on her side of the booth. She looked as if she were lost.

"Why would he ever do such a thing?" she asked.

"My brother?"

"Yes. What does he have to gain by prolonging his profits from a traditional sale?" Mackenzie asked.

Edmond leaned in, lowering his voice.

"If you ever get to a crossroads in life where you have to decide what's most important... your material possessions, or your health... I would like to think that you would choose the more valuable option of the two. Mackenzie, I think my brother has reached that point and he's making a wise decision to help someone else along the way. He's comfortable financially, and besides, it's not like you wouldn't be paying him his fair share."

Mack messaged her temples, chuckling in total disbelief.

"Well, I'll be. I certainly didn't see this coming."

"Hopefully, that's a positive thing," he said.

"It's not bad... but, oh man. It's going to take a minute for me to process the whole idea, that's for sure."

Edmond smiled... and again Mackenzie noticed

his white, neatly shaven beard. She observed something about his joy in delivering the message to her that was infectious.

"What about you? There's no part of you that would be interested in investing in a place like this?" she asked.

"Oh no. I'm a new retiree. I worked several years in corporate America, handling the finances for a fortune 500 company. Now... it's my time. Whether it be traveling, volunteering, or simply kicking up my feet. I'd like to have the choice of doing it at my leisure." He chuckled.

"Understood."

"How about I give you a little time to think things over? Let's say in a week or two we touch base, if that works for you."

"Uh... sure... a week or two." Mackenzie continued staring at the man in utter disbelief.

CHAPTER 13

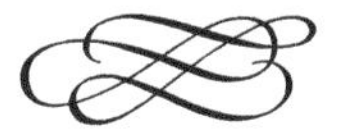

Early Friday morning, Mae sat with her daughter, soaking up the sound of laughter coming from her grandkids. She watched them play in their pj's near the Christmas tree, while Jonathan and Steven were on a mission to find peppermint flavored coffee, her daughter's holiday favorite.

"Lily, it's times like this that really make me wish we lived closer together. Look at my grandbabies. They're growing up way too fast for me. Even seeing you and Steven together just brings me so much joy," Mae said.

"I know, Mom. On one hand, I love that they're so independent. But I want time to slow down just a little, so I can take it all in. As for me and Steven, I tell him all the time how nice it is that I get to do life with my best friend. That's what it's really all about, isn't it?"

Lily and Steven were married straight out of college. She used to always tell stories of how they met on registration day at her beloved alma mater. He stood in the line catering to the first half of the alphabet, and she stood in the second line when they locked eyes. They both agree to this day that their encounter was love at first sight.

"I agree wholeheartedly. I felt that way about your father when he and I were starting the journey into parenthood. Trust me when I tell you, time flew by just as fast when you were an itty bitty thing. One minute I was carrying you in my belly, and the next you were off to prom. I nearly cried for days in between taking pictures of you and your date, Benjamin Walker," Mae replied.

"Oh, Mom. Please, not another Benjamin story. We were just friends from the neighborhood, and I only asked him because I didn't have anybody else to go with." Lily admitted.

"I know. But that poor boy sure had a crush on you. I'm just glad to know he finally got married and has kids of his own."

"Ha, you and all the other mothers in our community. You all were determined to fix him up with somebody from the neighborhood. I'll bet he was mortified." Lily chuckled.

"Maybe. But, it was all done with good intentions."

"Mmm hmm. Well... I know I've only been here a few days, but it's nice to see you and Jonathan as a married couple. You fit like a hand in glove, finishing each other's sentences, and of course, squabbling over the silliest things. All signs of two people who were made for each other."

"Thank you, dear. What you see is what you get with us. Building our friendship first really paid off. We needed that solid foundation before navigating marriage. I couldn't see it working any other way."

As they continued to speak, there was an abrupt knock at the front door.

"I wonder who that could be. Jonathan has his keys. Maybe it's my nosey neighbor, Meredith. The mere sight of a new car in our driveway is all it takes for her to ring the bell."

Mae walked to the front door, noticing someone holding a large Christmas package through the side window, blocking her view from seeing who it was. When she opened the door, she could see Jonathan and Steven standing in the background, but didn't recognize the hands, legs, or shoes of the foreign person standing at her doorstep.

"May I help you?" she asked.

Jonathan replied instead of the person holding the large box.

"Mae, I'd like to present to you Christmas gift

number two... a couple of days earlier than expected," he said.

They lowered the box to the ground, revealing the sight of her sister Rose on the other side. She spread her arms opened wide, greeting her sister with a big hug and a Merry Christmas, as if she were Santa Claus.

"Rose! Good gracious, I did not know that was you." Mae squealed.

The sisters squeezed each other, rocking from left to right out of pure excitement. When Mae could take a breath, she stood back, admiring Rose, and then pointed her finger at Jonathan.

"You knew my sister was coming early, and you didn't say one word, Jonathan. How many more tricks do you have up your sleeve? I don't know that I can take much more excitement." She smiled and reached out to hug Rose once more.

After a couple of hours of everyone enjoying each other's company, Jonathan gathered the family to hear the announcement he was about to make to his wife.

"Mae, hopefully the early arrival of our family explains why I urged you to take the morning off from work. There's a lot going on at Lighthouse Tours this week, and in just a little while, we'll join the festivities and help out. But, having this time with family is precious. Wouldn't you agree?" he asked.

"Jonathan, I'm speechless. Thank you for doing this. The next time I try to argue with you about taking time off, please ignore me."

"Gladly." Jonathan laughed, along with the family.

He inched closer toward Mae, taking her by the hand, lovingly addressing her before everyone in the living room.

"Mae, there's one more thing I'd like to do in order to make your gift complete," he said.

She stopped amid all the chuckles and looked at Jonathan.

"Jonathannnn. What else could you possibly be up to? I have my grandbabies, Lily, Steven, Rose... what more could I ask for?"

He smiled.

"Is there a brand new car in the driveway?" She teased.

"No. Our pickup will have to do for at least another year."

"Well, what is it? The suspense is killing me."

"I'd like to invite you to our official wedding ceremony. The one we never had. To be held this evening, in the chapel, right after the concert and festivities down at the gazebo," he replied.

"Say what?"

"We're getting married... again... and this time

we're going to do it right. Instead of gathering at the justice of peace, I'm giving you the wedding you and our loved ones always hoped for. That's why everyone came a few days early... they're here to celebrate Christmas and the renewing of our vows," he said.

"Are you serious?" she said, looking around at everyone in the room with her mouth wide open.

Mae's face turned flush red.

"After all this effort, to make sure everybody could attend. Including our family at Lighthouse Tours, and the café... I'm as a serious as a heart attack." Jonathan laughed.

"I... I..." Mae was stunned, struggling to find the words. The thought of Jonathan going to such effort caused tears to well up in her eyes.

"I don't know what to say," she replied.

Jonathan got down on one knee, holding a silver wedding band in his hand. It was simple, yet suitable to wear with her other rings if she chose to do so.

"Jonathan Middleton, I'll marry you one hundred times if that's what it takes to prove my love. There's only one thing I want to know," she said.

"What's that?"

"How on God's green earth am I supposed to have time to do my hair and prepare for such an event if we're going to be volunteering at Christmas Nights this evening?" She fussed.

The laughter among the family started all over

again, knowing that would be a major concern for Mae.

"Don't you worry. I've made arrangements for you to get all dolled up in the chapel before the ceremony. I know you well enough to make sure all the bases are covered." He smiled.

"Mom, I already knew Jonathan was a good man, but this just proves that he's a keeper," Lily said.

Mae's sister chimed in. "Any guy who's willing to renew their vows within the first year of marriage speaks volumes about their character. I can't even find a boyfriend, let alone a man who will marry me twice." Rose chuckled.

While Jonathan stood up to hug Mae, Steven couldn't resist jumping in.

"Hey, Jonathan, you're making guys like me look bad." He teased. Then he turned to Lily.

"I may not have a ring for you, babe. But, I found the peppermint coffee you like." He dangled the bag in the air, happily showing her how much he cared.

Jonathan continued to hug his wife gently, checking to make sure she was really okay with his spontaneous plans. "Are you sure you're up for this? I would understand if it's too much. I just wanted to do something special to surprise you... especially since you never seem to know what you want for Christmas." He smiled.

"I think it's a wonderful idea. I don't know how you come up with these things, Jonathan, but this is one surprise I'll never ever forget. Thank you," she said and slid her hand over his back, securely resting her head on his shoulder.

~

Clara glared at the clock, anxiously holding the fort down at Lighthouse Tours, while Mike headed to the airport to pick up his parents. What was supposed to be a peaceful evening of enjoying good Christmas music and getting well acquainted with his folks turned into a full night of festivities, including the Middletons' vowel renewal. According to Mike, his parents were excited and up for it, as they loved attending holiday events.

The gold bells hanging on the front door rang as Brody pushed through, entering with work bag in hand.

"Hey, Brody," she said.

"Good morning, Miss Clara... ready for the big day?"

"It depends on which part of the day you're referring to," she responded, biting her nails.

Clara sighed. "I'm meeting the Sanders for the first time, and I kid you not... I've been to the bathroom at least three times in the last hour. I think I'm allowing my nerves to get the best of me," she said, throwing her hands up.

"Why? You're all Mike ever talks about. If he

loves you that much, do you really think they're not going to love you as well?" he asked.

"Aww, Brody, that's so sweet."

"It's true."

"Yes, but there's something to be said about having that initial in person meeting and getting it behind you." She confessed.

The sound of the bells welcoming another guest into the store interrupted their conversation.

"Good morning, Ms. Covington." Logan Woods stood about six feet tall at the entrance with an air of confidence about him.

Clara signaled Brody to stay.

"Mr. Woods. To what do we owe the pleasure?" she asked.

"Ha... what a generous thing to say... if only it were true."

He let the door close behind him as he walked over to the front counter.

"I was wondering if Mike was free this morning. I came by to give him one last chance to reconsider my offer. I didn't expect to see the entire island rallying behind him on this Christmas Nights effort. It's a cute idea to be honest... but surely not one that will pay for the warehouse." He snickered.

"No one expects to pay for the whole thing. We're just trying to raise—"

Brody cut her off, not wanting to divulge their strategy.

"Mike is not in the office. Can we take a message for him?" he asked.

Woods looked Brody up and down before deciding to take him at his word.

"Yes. Forget mentioning anything to him about reconsidering my offer. That was an idea I had before I knew he and Mayor Thompson were behind this whole benefit concert. Mike Sanders must have some kind of hold on this island if he could go as far as getting everyone involved in such a charade." He snarled.

"It's not a charade, Logan. It's what people do when they love and support one another and when they have a heart for the greater good. Something you wouldn't know anything about," Clara replied.

"Hmm."

Brody moved closer to Clara's side. "Is there anything else we can do to help you? If not, I think it's best for you to be on your way," he said.

"No. Nothing else... at least not for today."

He turned around and slowly strutted toward the door.

Clara and Brody watched him quietly until he walked to his truck and pulled out of his parking space.

"Ughh, we should've seen that coming. I'm sure word about Christmas Nights hit him the minute he set foot on the island, sparking a flame of envy, of course," she said.

"That's not our problem. Our efforts to raise the money for the warehouse are fair. The residents here should have a choice instead of being bulldozed by the likes of Logan Woods. As for the warehouse, it's up to the owner who he sells to."

"I guess you're right. Besides, the clock is ticking and we're running out of time. We literally have this weekend, and the next... then that's it."

"Yep... have you heard the latest on how much we've raised so far?"

Clara checked the spreadsheet that both she and Jan were keeping tabs on.

"We're just shy of seven thousand, which is up fifteen-hundred dollars from last week," she said, trying to sound chipper, even though they had quite a long way to go.

"Hey, we still need to be thankful for the progress. Seven thousand dollars is nothing to sneeze at. The word I'm hearing is the business owners couldn't be more pleased with the additional traffic this year. As for the rest, all we can do is be hopeful. Now is certainly not the time for giving up... no matter what Logan says."

CHAPTER 14

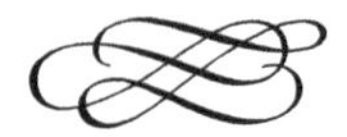

"Ag, don't look now, but rumor has it there's a new guy in town who's been admiring you from afar. They say he's an author... and I think that's him, standing to the left of the gazebo. I've already seen him checking you out at least twice since we've been here," Clara said.

"Nope. Sorry. No can do. I already declared a vow to take a year off and I'm not going back on my word now. Eh eh. Besides, I'm this close to pulling everything together for my food truck next spring. The last thing I have time for is a man," she replied adamantly, facing the opposite direction.

"Hey, I'm on your team. That's exactly what I said to the ladies at the café when they told me about him, but as your sister I figured I should still let you know," Clara said.

"Great. So, now I'm the talk of the café?"

"No, of course not. He is. Everybody thinks he's cute, but we all want to know his story. Supposedly, he's renting a beach house on the island. But, I wonder what he writes, and does he write under a pseudonym? It's all kind of mysterious, but interesting at the same time, don't you think?" she asked.

"I don't have an opinion about it, really. Maybe he's seeking an escape from reality if he came out here to rent a beach house. He's probably in search of some peace and quiet. Either way, I'm leaving all the curiosity up to you guys. I have a busy job and a business to start... and how soon we forget... my last relationship didn't exactly go that well... remember?"

"Oh, I remember all right," Clara said, drawing in a long breath as she skimmed the crowd.

Agnes continued. "There's a bite in the air this evening. Perhaps one perk of living off the water, I suppose?"

"If you think this is cold, just wait until we hit January and February. Maybe this year we'll get lucky and have at least one or two inches of snow."

"I'll pass. Nestling up by the fireplace while watching the ripples form in the Patuxent is good enough for me. We shoveled enough snow back in New York to last a lifetime. I'm good."

"Ha, I'll bet." Clara continued searching the crowd, almost standing on her tippy toes, looking for Mike.

"Hey, aren't you supposed to be meeting your in-laws right about now?"

"Yep. Mike left the shop early to change and head for the airport. As usual, he said he encountered a lot of traffic, but they should pull up any moment now. I think he wanted to give them time to put their things down at his place and freshen up before heading over," she said.

"Yikes, what a long day for them."

"I thought the same, but he says they're up for it. Apparently, they're excited to help volunteer tonight, and they're even willing to tag along to Jonathan and Mae's ceremony. It's a rather sweet gesture, don't you think?"

"I do. Are you nervous?" Agnes asked.

"A little, but more excited than anything else. Just ready to get the show on the road, if you will."

Agnes pointed to the front of the crowd. "Well, speaking of getting the show on the road, Clay Nathan is taking the stage. I'll bet within a minute of him singing the first note, one of these women are bound to fall out, right here on the lawn of the gazebo." She giggled.

"He does have a way about him, that's for sure."

Agnes nodded. "I thought surely we'd have to call an ambulance the last time he sang I'll Be Home for Christmas."

As Clay pulled the first few strings of his guitar,

welcoming the crowd, he thanked them for being a part of the benefit concert and began humming a tune. Clara felt a quick tug on her waistline and turned around to the sight of Mike and his parents.

"Oh, my gosh. You made it." She squealed.

Mrs. Sanders held her arms out, gesturing for Clara to come toward her.

"Mrs. Sanders, it's so nice to meet you in person," Clara said, giving her a hug. She closed her eyes for a moment, breathing in her perfume and recalling fond memories of when her mother used to hold her just so.

"Please, call me Barbara. You're even more stunning in person. Just look at you," she replied.

Mr. Sanders approached the two with a jolly demeanor. "Ah, my future daughter-in-law," he said, holding his arms open wide. "We're big huggers in this family. I hope you don't mind."

"Are you kidding?" She embraced him and again felt that familiar warmth that only comes from a parent.

Relief painted over Clara's face. Without having spent much time together, she loved the way they drew her in. As if she were already carrying the last name Sanders.

"Oh, I almost forgot. This is my sister, Agnes.... Ag... this is Barbara and Mr.—"

Mike's dad interrupted, ensuring Clara that he

also wanted to be addressed by his first name. "Please, call me Rich."

Agnes gladly stepped forward, doing her best to represent her sister well. "It's a pleasure meeting you. I've heard nothing but wonderful things from my sister about you. I'm just glad the day has finally come that you all could get together. Looks like you arrived just in time for Clay Nathan," she yelled, trying to speak over the roaring of the crowd.

Mike slid between Clara and his parents. "I called Mayor Thompson on the way over here. We agreed to take the stage during a brief intermission to update everyone on where we are with the fundraiser and to thank them for their support. Do you think you guys will be okay here while I go handle a few things?" he asked.

"We'll be just fine. I already feel as if I've known Rich and Barb forever. If you want, I can get them acquainted with the volunteer post that we have set up," she said.

"That would be wonderful, Clara. Rich and I are ready to get our hands dirty for a good cause," Barb said.

Clara remembered all the anxiety she once felt at the thought of meeting Mike's parents. Now, they were here, strolling side-by-side with her down Main Street, taking in the Christmas sights and sounds.

"So, what do you think about Christmas Nights so far? Pretty spectacular, isn't it?" she asked.

"Oh, Clara, it's absolutely gorgeous. Mike tells us you two coordinated with the residents and owners to pull this altogether. It's absolutely amazing," Barbara said.

Rich pointed to a mechanical snowman in the window of one store while they spoke.

"Trust me, it was quite the undertaking, but with everyone's help, somehow we pulled it off. I think everyone just has a heart for Christmas out here... and maybe an even bigger heart for Lighthouse Tours," she said, shining a light on Mike and his hard work.

Rich stopped. "Tell me about it. He's been keeping us abreast of all the latest happenings with this big wig... what's his name again?"

"Logan Woods," she said.

"That's him, all right. Who does he think he is? I mean... come on, for goodness' sake. It's a free country. The man has a right to inquire about starting a business here. But, to threaten Mike the way he has and to bombard his way in as if he plans to operate some sort of monopoly is unacceptable. I say good for the people of Solomons to do everything they can to put a stop to it." He emphasized.

Barb held up one finger.

"And, I might be biased as his mother, but Mike is a better fit for running a boat storage facility for Solomons Island," she said.

"I agree. The business will be represented by familiar names the people can trust. I just hope we can raise enough money to make this happen. Mike is already generously volunteering to use some of his current funds to bring the warehouse up to speed, but the down payment has to come from somewhere. He can't do it all by himself."

Barbara patted Clara on the back as they continued to stroll. "Don't you worry. These things always have a way of working out for the best. Isn't that right, Rich?" she asked, glancing at her husband.

"One hundred percent," he replied.

They continued walking, almost reaching the volunteer post near the chapel where Jonathan and Mae were scheduled to renew their vows. Everyone was busy doing their part for the evening and was scheduled to meet around the nine o'clock hour.

"So, Clara. We've been eager to know more about you. Mike is clearly head over heels in love. You don't know how happy that makes me. It's been a long time since I've heard him talk about anybody the way he does you. From the moment you met, leading to the proposal. I think we knew it was love before he did... or at least before he was willing to admit it." She chuckled.

Clara revealed a shy smile. She wished she knew Barb back then. Hearing a mother's perspective as she watched her son fall in love may have served as a confirmation of their growing feelings for each other. Thankfully, things worked out just the same.

"It was definitely a whirlwind... but a good one, if you will. I think if Mike and I had to do it all over again, we would've pursued a personal relationship from the start... not involving work amid our budding feelings for one another. But, hey- I guess you can't plan these things. You can't always be prepared for everything that comes your way," Clara said.

She noticed Rich and Barb were harmonious together in everything they did. The way they walked, spoke to one another... they showed obvious signs of a couple who'd been married for over fifty years.

"I wasn't ready when I met Barb. I had just completed my shift for the day, and when I saw her entering the vestibule where I worked, I nearly got the wind knocked out of me. I literally gasped for air." He laughed.

"Oh, stop it, Rich. Nobody wants to hear a sappy story about how two old people fell in love."

"I do." Clara raised her hand.

Talking about your love story is wayyy better than me talking about my life, Clara thought.

Rich checked with Barb before divulging his version of the story.

"Oh, go ahead," she said, encouraging him.

He held out his hand as if painting the scene. Clara loved how vibrant and fun they were. In a lot of ways, she was thankful they were going to be her in-laws. She had always heard war stories from other brides, but in her case, it felt like she hit the jackpot.

"We worked in two glass buildings, side by side with a bridge that connected one to the other. I worked in the software department, and Barb worked for the same company over in payroll. Unbeknownst to me, the mail for our department would occasionally get delivered to hers. It was an honest mistake that even the best delivery person could make."

Barb cleared her throat. "I'm not so sure about that. Only one building had a payroll department. How confusing could it be?" She shrugged her shoulders.

"Barb... Barb... Barb... how many times do I have to tell you—"

"It was fate," they said in unison.

"That's correct. It was fate and you know it. It was meant to be that on Thursday, November 20, 1960... you would come walking down my hall, asking for me by name." Rich smiled.

"You're right, dear. I asked for you by name... and you didn't waste any time asking me out on a lunch date," Barb replied.

She turned to Clara. "Of course, I turned him down several times before finally giving in. I knew nothing about him, and until I had time to do some investigating, it was a no go for me," she said.

"But, I pursued her... and pursued her... and pursued her until she finally caved."

By now, Clara had stopped at the front staircase of the chapel, holding her hands together in a praying position, swept away by their love story.

"That's so sweet. There's nothing like a man that knows what he wants," Clara said.

"Yep, and here we are all these years later, still going strong," Barb responded.

"You'll have to promise me I get to hear more during your visit."

"Likewise, Clara. We want to hear more about you as well. But, for now, is this our post for collecting donations?" Barb asked.

"Yes, it is. Are you sure you want to do this? Especially after such a long day of traveling and being in traffic?"

"Clara, we have from now until Christmas to be lazy bums while we visit with you and Mike. We can't think of any place we'd rather be right now than helping with such a good cause."

"Okay. Well, I'll grab your buckets. I believe they left a few stored behind the doorway. In just about an hour, we'll send other volunteers to swap places and give you a break."

"It sounds good. Barb, you can stay here near the

church, and I can go across the street, catching the crowd heading in the opposite direction," Rich said.

Mike's pretty lucky to have such nice folks. Correction. Both you and Mike are lucky, Clara thought to herself and walked away with a sense of belonging she hadn't experienced since her parents were alive.

CHAPTER 15

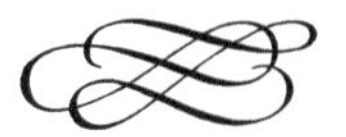

"Brody, look at those two, standing up there, glowing as if they didn't have a care in the world besides each other. Aren't they beautiful?" Mackenzie said, tapping him on the arm. She admired them as they stood at the front of the chapel, hand in hand with Jonathan, reciting their vows.

"They do look amazing. Almost as if they've been preparing for this all day. I can hardly tell they were just volunteering at the gazebo a little while ago," he replied.

"I know. I want to be just like Mae and Jonathan when I get to be their age. You can tell they really put their love first, and they're committed to being adventurous together. That's the way to do it. Life's too short to let it pass you by, living day in and day out, only indulging in the mundane."

She whispered as they sat toward the back in a private section of their own. Mack couldn't contain her excitement for the Middletons. If she were being honest, part of the joy she felt was the unknown about where her future would lead with Brody.

"Have you ever thought about what your ideal wedding would be like? I would imagine you'd want something different from what you had the first time around with Stephanie's father." Brody inquired, while waving at a few of the guests he recognized from Lighthouse Tours.

"It may be hard to believe, but I didn't have a grand wedding like one may expect. We were too broke to pay for such a thing. But, if I had to do it all over again, I'd still have a small ceremony, very much like this one. It's the intimacy for me... there's nothing like sharing something this special with close friends and family. Greeting them all one-by-one, and actually having time to spend with each of them." She laughed.

"And time to eat your meal," he said.

"Yep, that, too. I hear so many stories about brides and grooms who never have time to eat the night of their wedding. That wouldn't be me. I get way too hangry for that nonsense."

Brody covered his mouth, holding back an outburst of laughter at Mackenzie's candidness. It was one of the things he'd come to love about her.

"Hey, you can laugh all you want, but it's the

truth. The one thing you'll never have to worry about with me is trying to figure out how I feel. I'll eliminate all the guesswork for you. Especially when it comes to being hungry... and when it comes to being too tired as well. Even though, after having Stephanie, there is no such thing as being too tired. I just drink coffee now more than ever." She rambled.

"I'll have to keep that in mind."

The two simmered down their conversation as they listened to the pastor recite scripture over the recommitment of their vows to one another. Clara listened to every word and took in the beauty of the poinsettias decorating the end of each pew, the Christmas wreaths hanging in the windows, and the purple drapery hanging just so on the cross in front of them.

Brody leaned in to whisper once more.

"I think the next time around you should plan a special ceremony... one fit for a queen. No matter how old we get, our childhood dreams always live within us, you know. Wouldn't it be nice if you could fulfill yours?"

She placed her hand in his, intertwining their fingers together.

"Agreed. I like the way you think, Brody. I have so many dreams I'd like to fulfill. Maybe it's time I start making a list and checking them off one by one."

"What are some of your other dreams?"

"You really want to know?" she whispered.

She motioned for them to wait until the pastor announced the Middletons' recommitment to one another. They watched Jonathan and Mae kiss, then walked down the aisle hand in hand. They cheered with the crowd as the happy couple passed by, exiting the chapel.

"Okay, now tell me," Brody said, turning to face Mack. "Name a few of your dreams that you want to add to the list."

"You really want to know right now?" she asked.

"Of course, I do. Tell me... what's your top three?"

Mack bit her lip.

"Okay, but you have to swear to secrecy, and you can't make fun of me... no matter how silly it may seem," she replied.

"Never."

She drew in a breath, looking around to make sure no one had reached their pew yet.

"I want to remarry... the right man this time, of course. I'd love to send Steph to the best college of her choosing someday. I want to become the next owner of the cafe, and I'd like to learn how to crochet. The last one not being as serious, but you asked—" she replied with a nervous chuckle.

He stared at her. Not in a weird way, more like in amazement.

"What? Say something, already. This is making me feel vulnerable," she said playfully.

"I think your list is wonderful... and honestly, there's not one goal you've mentioned so far that you can't achieve. I'll bet it's all within arm's reach."

"Well, I don't know about the crocheting. I used to watch my grandmother crochet for hours. She made the most beautiful blankets you ever did see. My one or two attempts to make a winter scarf were absolutely pathetic." Mack smiled.

"Okay, so you'll practice some more."

"For sure. But, in the meantime, at least one of those goals may be attainable this week. Well... technically, I could at least take the initial steps if I wanted to," she said.

"Surely you're not referring to Steph going to college or getting married this week... unless you know something I don't."

"Noo, silly." She smiled.

"Did you sign up for a class to learn to crochet?"

"Not yet. It's the café. The owner is waiting for me to decide if I want to sign a lease-to-own agreement." She hesitated, feeling uncertain as to whether it was the right thing to do or to say aloud. What if people thought she was good enough to manage the place, but not to own it? What if she couldn't hold up her end of the deal with the lease-to-own agreement? These were all important things to be considered — and maybe even worry about.

Clara popped her head in between them, waving to the budding couple she adored as a duo.

"Hey, guys, I didn't realize you were sitting just a few pews behind us. You should've joined us up front." She smiled.

"We would've, but we arrived late. Don't you look pretty," Mack said, brushing out a ruffle on the shoulder of Clara's dress.

"Thanks. It was all I could pull together at the last minute. If you guys have a second, I'd love to introduce you to Mike's parents. They're right over here."

Mack and Brody stepped forward toward Mike's parents, putting on their most welcoming smile, but Mack knew before the evening was over, she had to get feedback from Brody. Was she about to make the right choice? She needed to hear something other than her own thoughts swarming around in her head. Some form of confirmation to either propel her to sign on the dotted line or head for the hills.

Later that evening at the Middletons', Mae slipped in the bedroom, closing the door gently behind her. It had been an exciting yet exhausting day. After their small reception at the chapel, it was all she could do but kick off her slippers and lay flat on her back next to Jonathan. *I just need five minutes,* she told herself while easing on to the covers. If only she could manage to lie down without waking Jonathan up.

"I'll bet you're worn out. Aren't you, darlin?" he asked, waking up out of a snore.

"Jonathan, you nearly startled me to death. With the way you were snoring one would think you're the one who's worn out," she said, poking fun at him.

"I was just resting my eyes momentarily. I thought maybe if I snuck in a little power nap, then I could recharge for a little snuggle time with my honey," he said, rolling over, inching closer to Mae.

She interlocked arms with him, resting her eyelids as she spoke.

"Jonathan."

"Hmm."

"What you did for me tonight... for us... was truly something special. Not that the family ever doubted our love, but did you see the looks on their faces... the joy that came from hearing us recommit to one another? Even the grandkids were happy to play a role by lighting the candles. I'll never forget tonight. I will forever etch it in my heart," she said.

"Well, I sure hope you don't forget it. Especially after all the hoops we had to jump through to plan this without you knowing about it." He chuckled. "And, hopefully, you can better appreciate why I did things the way I did. I planned the ceremony before Christmas so we could spend the rest of the time together with the family."

"Yes, my love. It was so well thought out. You didn't miss a beat."

"Well... technically, there was one thing that almost got in the way. At the time we arranged the schedule, we had no idea we would be right smack in the middle of everything going on with Christmas Nights. But Lily was right. She said it would serve as an excellent distraction for you, and it did. It darn near wore us both out," he said, laughing himself into a little coughing spell.

"I love my sweet daughter, but in her mind, she must think I'm Super Woman. I'm not as young as I used to be. There was a lot going on today. But, in hindsight, I wouldn't have changed a thing. Now, as long as I can lift my limbs in the morning, then we can all have a decent breakfast to start our day."

"Don't worry about it, Mae. Lily and Rose have it covered. We've been given strict instructions to sleep in while the grands help them prepare breakfast."

"Oh, that sounds heavenly," she said, drifting in and out of the sweetest snooze, resting in each other's arms.

"Jonathan?"

"Yes, dear."

"I love you."

"I love you more, Mae... I love you more."

Brody sat with his truck running idle in front of Mackenzie's apartment building. He turned the knob, cranking up the heat another degree, watching as a few snowflakes melted on the windshield, then quickly turning over to rain.

"I didn't hear anything about a wintry mix in the forecast, did you?" she asked.

"No, but it probably won't amount to much. I think the temperature is supposed to rise above freezing by the morning."

"That's too bad. Steph has been praying for snow. She's been following all the old wives' tales to generate her first snow day... wearing her pj's inside out... doing the snow dance... you name it. It's funny to watch and see what she'll come up with next." Mack smiled.

"She's creative and has an adventurous spirit just like her mother. For some it takes a lifetime to figure out how to find joy in the little things."

"That's so true. May she never lose her appreciation for the little things," Mackenzie said, looking up toward her daughter's window. The lights were turned off at such a late hour. All she could see were flashing lights from the television that played in the living room where her babysitter would normally sit.

Brody reached his hand over, removing strands of hair behind Mack's shoulder blade.

"Not that you ever needed to hear this from me... but you are more than capable of owning the café. You are the heartbeat of that place, Mackenzie."

"No, the customers are the heartbeat. I, on the

other hand, just make sure the place stays afloat. It's been part of my struggle over these last few days, trying to figure out if I'd really be good at this, or if I'm just kidding myself," she responded.

He shifted himself to address her face to face.

"Really? Where is that confident and tenacious spirit you normally possess? I can understand if the idea of embarking upon something new is a little frightening, but you can't let that stop you."

She noticed more snowflakes forming, then dissolving on the windshield.

"How are you so confident about my abilities, Brody? I mean... we're continuously getting to know each other and it's going great, if I might add... but what makes you so sure?" she asked.

"I sense it on the inside of me. I see you in action every single day, serving your customers with so much love, and they keep coming back for more. I feel pretty confident that the café will fill up with customers tomorrow morning, wanting more of Harold's good food. It's a place to gather family and friends, and they will overwhelmingly ask for you and would miss you if you weren't there. Why? It's because in their minds you already possess the position of owner. The only thing that's left for you to do is step into your role and own it," he said.

She let out a deep breath.

"Wow. After putting it like that—"

"There's not much left to wonder or question, is there?" he asked.

"Not really. I mean... it's probably a wise idea for me to find an accountant who can look things over and make sure the numbers look good with the lease... maybe they could even set me up on some sort of plan to make sure we stay financially strong as a business. But-"

Brody waited.

"But- I guess you're right. I don't know what I've been fretting over. Everything I've ever wanted in terms of having a business of my own has been carefully orchestrated and laid out before me. I might be a little nervous, but that's normal. Overall, I think this is my time," she said, turning to look him in the eyes.

"There's the Mackenzie I know and love. You've got this."

She lowered her eyes and whispered softly, "Thank you, Brody."

He tilted her chin up, brushing his lips with hers delicately, which she gladly reciprocated. The sweet taste of his lips caused her to shiver, which she tried so hard to control. She may not have spoken the words yet, but her body language screamed that she, too, was falling deeply and hopelessly in love.

"Brody, you don't know how much this means to me," she whispered over the sound of her heart racing a mile a minute.

"Me kissing you?" He smiled.

"No, even though that's nice, too. But, I mean having your support. It's been a busy season with everything going on and... I needed somebody to talk to. Thank you for listening to me and for not shooting my dreams down."

"Never. Mackenzie, I would never do such a thing. You can always come to me with anything, and I will always be your biggest cheerleader, supporting you every step of the way." He promised.

"Always?"

"Always. As in... forever. I guess that means you and Stephanie are stuck with me." He chuckled.

"Hmm... stuck with you. That sounds like a good thing to me."

CHAPTER 16

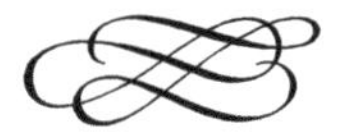

"Ladies and gentlemen," Mayor Thompson announced on the microphone. He stood in front of the grand Christmas tree amid snowflakes that swirled, falling more steadily than the previous evening.

"On behalf of myself and the employees of Lighthouse Tours, I'd like to welcome you to the last weekend of Christmas Nights, shopping, concerts, and more. I hope that you've enjoyed taking in the sights of the decorated streets, and that you've shopped to your heart's content. Before we bring Clay Nathan to the stage again, I'd like to give you an update on where we are with the fundraiser. As you know, we've been collecting donations to help benefit the purchase and grand opening of a storage warehouse for our boats. A facility that Lighthouse Tours would operate. By the way, how many of you have enjoyed the decorated boats and phenomenal parade put on by Mike and his team?" he said, encouraging the crowd's support.

He could hear cheers and whistles across the gazebo and down the dock for miles.

"At this time, Miss Jan and Miss Clara Covington will present our donation tracker to show us where we are with the numbers. Ladies," he announced.

Jan, the secretary from North Beach and Clara, rolled out a large thermometer projecting their goal of twenty thousand dollars at the top, with their current status of thirteen thousand shaded in red.

Everyone clapped, but it was clear they still had a way to go if they were going to reach their goal by the end of the month.

Mayor Thompson continued to speak.

"To the residents and visitors of Solomons Island, look what you've been able to do," he said, pointing to the chart. "A huge thank you, from the bottom of our hearts. We are currently at thirteen thousand dollars, which is no small number by any means. Seeing everybody working together for such a good cause and giving when it's really a time that most of us have to focus on purchasing for the family... well... it's heartwarming... and we truly appreciate your love and support."

On the sidelines Clara returned to standing by Mike and his parents as they continued to listen to Mayor Thompson speak.

"Before Clay plays for us, I believe Mike Sanders has prepared something he'd briefly like to share."

This time Tommy and Brody rolled out a big chart displaying an architectural image of what he hoped the warehouse could become in the near future.

"Let's give it up one more time for the residents and tourists of Solomons," Mike said, cheering the crowd on.

When the crowd settled, he continued.

"The folks over at Lighthouse Tours have been quite busy this week... some of us volunteering, others composing a remodeling plan, and amid it all some of us even renewing our vows," he said, pointing to Jonathan and Mae, to which they received a loud cheer.

"Through it all, we hope to provide you with everything you've been asking for and more. We present to you a visual display of our plans for a full boat storage, keeping in mind that we will also offer you an annual Christmas Nights spectacular event including decorated streets and a boat parade run by Lighthouse Tours."

Everyone began clapping and chanting Lighthouse Tours... Lighthouse Tours... Lighthouse Tours.

"We've even made a little deal with our dear friend, Clay Nathan, to return next year. Isn't that right Clay?"

Clay stood several feet to the side, tipping his hat with his guitar strapped across his winter jacket. He wore a cowboy hat and jeans and, of course, the slightest gesture made the ladies go wild.

"Thank you, Clay. We appreciate all that you're doing for us. Solomons, we'll leave this laminated blueprint further down the dock for everyone to see at their own leisure. Thanks for all that you've done and in advance for all that you will do to help make the dream of raising twenty thousand dollars a reality. Together, we can make it happen. With that being said... ladies and gentlemen, the man we've all been waiting for... Clay Nathannnnnnn. Enjoy Christmas Nights, everybody!"

Mike cleared the stage, joining his loved ones on a walk toward the offices of Lighthouse Tours.

The next day, Mae stood at the threshold of her door, watching Meredith's eyes as they switched from looking at her to looking beyond where she was standing. She smiled, slightly adjusting the door open so she could satisfy her curiosity.

"How are you, Meredith?"

"I'm well, thank you. I see you have your hands full," she replied, continuing to glance beyond Mae's shoulder.

"Yes, my sister is here along with Lily, her husband, and the grandkids. Just a little family gathering for Christmas, that's all."

"I see. Well, that explains why you missed the big announcement," she replied.

"What announcement? We've been down to the gazebo just about every day for Christmas Nights. I don't think we missed anything."

"I'm referring to the neighborhood decorating contest. We announced the winners yesterday afternoon, and I sent you an email. With all the cars in your driveway, I figured you didn't have a chance to check it, so I decided to come by. It turns out you and Jonathan won third place... I won second, and get this... the Zimmermans actually came in at first place. Who would've ever thought at the eleventh hour they'd step up and steal the number one spot?" she said, waving around her one-fingered mitten.

"Ha — Oh, Meredith, I hardly think it's fair to call it a steal if they won fair and square." Mae laughed.

"Yes, but I was certainly temped to ask for a recount. I mean, come on, really? Number one? Their decorations were homemade just like everyone else's. No offense, but they completely overlooked the detail and work of art at my place... starting with the precisely aligned lightbulbs along the A-line of the roof, down to the candy cane trimmed driveway," she said, shaking her head.

"Meredith — you still won. It may not be first place, but your name is still on the list. Besides, look at the good that came out of all this. I'll bet the Zimmerman children had a blast helping their parents decorate. It probably brought cheer to a household that would otherwise be focused on a divorce, and it brought the neighborhood together. It was a win for everybody if you ask me," Mae said, trying to console her, even though she really didn't feel an ounce of pity.

Meredith shifted her stance.

"I guess you're right. Besides, I really can't consume the first-place prize of hot chocolate, anyway. All the dairy gives me hot flashes for at least an hour after consumption and causes me to run straight to the—" She stopped mid-sentence.

It was all Mae could do to keep her composure.

Poor child, Mae thought.

"Well, I guess I'll head back over to my side of the fence. Say hello to the family for me," Meredith said, turning around.

"Uh, Meredith. Hold on a second."

"Yes."

"What are your plans for the holidays? I know you mentioned your son recently accepted a new job.

Does that mean you don't have plans for Christmas?" she asked.

"Oh, you know how it goes with the younger generation. They're so busy traveling here, there, and everywhere. I didn't want to be a burden by putting too much pressure on him to come. I have plenty to do around the house to keep me busy."

"Like what?" Mae asked.

"You know, the list of chores is endless. I'll just play my favorite black and white movies and fiddle around." She waved like it was no big deal.

"Meredith. Nobody I know worries about doing chores on Christmas Day or New Year's for that matter. If you want, you're more than welcome to come over and enjoy a meal with us." Mae offered.

"At your place?" Meredith responded, seeming surprised.

"That's normally where we eat."

Mae figured she was probably surprised. Technically, she was breaking their normal cadence of bantering back and forth. A cardinal rule they strictly adhered to most days of the year. But if she couldn't open her doors and extend herself for Christmas, then what good would it be to call herself a neighbor?

"So — what do you say? I'm making string bean casserole and my sister is a master baker — pecan pie being at the top of her list," Mae said, cracking a smile.

"Well, I guess I can put my culinary skills to use.

I make a mean Christmas ham wrapped in puff pastry. Do you think your folks would enjoy that?"

"Will they? Don't be surprised if they clear the serving tray... and don't say I didn't warn you." Mae chuckled.

Meredith smiled, relaxing her stance a little.

"Mae, thank you. I'm looking forward to it."

Mae winked at her. "Me, too."

They retreated, each going their separate ways for the evening. Mae pushed the door closed and turned the bottom lock. On the way to the kitchen she yelled, "Honeyyy, guess who's coming to Christmas dinnerrrr." She chuckled to herself.

"Hi, may I have a large latte to go, please?" Agnes said, while peering through the glass encasement, glossing over the desserts.

At the coffee shop, there were a few evening stragglers on their laptops. Some browsing magazines over a hot brew, others simply chatting.

"Hey, I think I'll add the apple strudel to my order, if you don't mind. Can you heat it up just a tad for me?" she asked.

Harvey, the cashier, scooped up the dessert, explaining it would be about a five-minute wait.

"Thank you."

"No problem," he replied.

As she rubbed her hands together to keep warm, a deep and rather rugged voice spoke up from close behind.

"It's worth the wait."

She whipped around, partially startled that someone would even stand so close and partially agitated. Back in the city where she was from, if you stood too close you could get knocked into next week — no questions asked.

"Excuse me?" she said, immediately noticing the drop dead, gorgeous man standing before her with a cup in hand. Her heart began thumping to the rhythm of an imaginary jackhammer.

"The apple strudel... it's delicious. Definitely worth waiting the five extra minutes to heat it up," he said, as he inched back, presumably reading her body language.

Man, this guy is hot, she thought.

"Oh, yeah. Right. The apple strudel. Yes — I figured I would try it. I probably don't need all the sugar, but, oh well... what the heck," she replied.

Okay, now you're babbling.

Silence fell between them as they continued staring awkwardly at one another.

"Are you from around here?" she asked, breaking the silence.

"No. I'm here for a project. I guess you can call it a short-term assignment, if you will. It should last about three months, max. How about yourself?"

"Me? Oh, no. I'm from New York. I'm currently living with my sister while I try to get on my feet. Not that I'm not on my feet financially. I have a job, but I'm working on starting a small business, and you know how that can be." She rambled.

Whoa, you just divulged half of your life story to a complete stranger. Will you exercise some control? she thought.

"That sounds interesting. Hey, if I'm not mistaken, I think I've seen you before. Were you at the Clay Nathan concert at the gazebo yesterday?" he asked.

She crossed her arms, folded over her chest to keep from being too fidgety.

"Yes, I was there."

"I thought so... my name is Grant." He extended his hand.

She caught a whiff of his cologne, causing her to nearly become delusional. Thankfully, Harvey snapped her out of her fog by yelling, "Apple strudel ready on the counter."

"Uh, Grant. Nice to meet you." She stuttered, then reached around to get her dessert.

"So — what did you say you do again? Did you mention you were here on a temporary assignment?" she asked.

"Yes. I'm an author. Solomons Island just happens to be the perfect place for me to conduct a little research for my next book... soooo... here I am. I'm renting a place not too far from here."

"Oh. I see," she replied.

Disappointment washed over her as she recalled the conversation with Clara. The one where she didn't want to become the talk of the town and where she was way too busy planning for her start up to date anyone.

You're supposed to be on a one-year sabbatical. Remember? she thought.

"Well, you picked a wonderful time of year to observe the island. There's certainly plenty to do and plenty to see," she said.

"Yes, it's perfect here. Very coastal. I love it," he said, rocking back and forth on his heels. He, too, appeared to have a bit of a nervous twitch, but she couldn't allow herself to read too far into it.

Agnes broke the connection between their eyes and pushed the image of his perfect smile out of her mind. Instead, she drew in the smell of her apple strudel, slightly lifting it to her nose.

"Mmm, I guess I'd better try the strudel before it gets cold. It was nice meeting you, Mr. —" she said.

"Grant... please, call me Grant."

"Right. Grant. It was nice meeting you."

"Heading out so soon?" he asked.

"Yep, I have somewhere that I need to be. I hope you enjoy your stay on Solomons Island," she replied.

He barely had time to respond before she placed a twenty-dollar bill on the counter, letting Harvey know he could keep the change. She offered one last friendly nod, lifting her coffee cup to wave goodbye, and walked away, determined to shake the goosebumps he was giving her and stay focused on her sabbatical.

CHAPTER 17

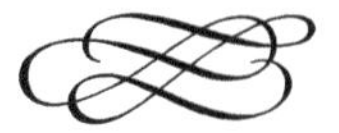

Clara placed her serving tray filled with cookies on the coffee table, leaving room for Barb to set her famous eggnog down. Mike and his father were still camping out in front of the television, making it convenient for the ladies to sneak away and catch up.

"Clara, I know Mike mentioned a while back you inherited this place, but he didn't come close to preparing me for what to expect. This house looks like something out of a Christmas card. How in the world do you keep up with it all?" Barb asked.

"Honestly, I think my former profession has a lot to do with it. I may have changed careers, but I don't think I could ever lose the knack for cleaning and staying organized. It's a part of my DNA." She smiled.

"Well, in that case, can I take you back home with me?" Barb teased.

"Sure, anytime." She chuckled.

"Seriously, with a place this big, you had to have hired some help by now."

"No. It's just me and my sister Agnes, who sends her regards, by the way. I think she wanted to give us some time to get acquainted, but I know she'll be joining us for Christmas dinner," Clara replied.

"Please tell her that wasn't necessary. We're all family now, which means she should be included. Mike mentioned that she's been living here with you for a few months now which made me happy to hear. I'd hate to think you were living here all by yourself."

"I know it may seem strange, but I'm actually not afraid to be here. Having Agnes around has been a bonus, but well before we established our living arrangement, I was used to being here for Joan, my boss... at least until she passed away, that is."

"Oh, Clara. I'm so sorry for your loss. You must've been very close to Joan... and she must've thought highly of you," Barb said, waving her hand to showcase the grandeur of her surroundings.

"Thank you. We were like family to one another. It's one reason I've yet to consider selling. I know the logical thing to do would be to downsize, but I can't. I just can't give up the memories. Packing up and leaving would be too painful."

"I'll bet. The good news is no one would ever expect you to do so if it's not how you're being led. Especially not Mike. He doesn't care if you lived in his small cottage or in a mansion on a hilltop somewhere… he just wants to be with you. Trust me, he's expressed it to us several times." She smiled.

"That's so sweet."

Barb passed Clara a glass of eggnog.

"Thank you. Maybe I should get a fire going for us? It might be nice to enjoy a little warmth from the wood-burning stove." Clara offered.

"That would be nice, but I'm sure the guys wouldn't mind helping us. I'd love to just sit here and spend some time with you — I have so many questions, I don't know where to begin."

Oh dear, Clara thought.

"For example. I'm dying to know about the wedding… have you two set a specific date yet? The time of year sets the tone for everything else. Wedding colors, the venue, indoor versus outdoor. The list is endless."

Clara raised her hand.

"I'll confess that I'm the reason we've been undecided thus far. But, I'm really not that picky. As long as Mike agrees, I could get married any time of the year. We could get married as early as two or three months from now. That's plenty of time to find a dress."

"When?" Barb asked.

"The spring. Maybe even a little earlier?"

"Oh. In that case, you have your work cut out for you. Either way, the most important thing is the two of you are happy. That's all that matters, and don't let anyone tell you anything different."

Clara released a quiet sigh. Barb's supportive nature was just what she needed. Especially since she no longer had the support of her own mother in well over a decade.

"Hey, Barb."

"Yes."

"I'm sure Mike had to mention something to you about my parents being deceased." Clara hesitated.

"He did. Although, just barely touching the surface. He respects you and thought it would be best that we talk about these kinds of things whenever you were comfortable bringing it up. Not to say that time has to be now."

"It's okay. My parents and I were very close. We used to talk to each other every single night, which may sound crazy to some... maybe even a little much, given that I was married at the time of their passing. But it didn't matter. You never stop being Daddy's little girl... and mom's little girl," she said, with moisture clouding her vision.

Clara continued. "This time of year was very special to us. I can almost close my eyes and envision mom making sure the gifts were stacked under the tree just so. And, every year, it never failed... she would place several gifts under the tree and still manage to forget several others in various hiding places all around the house." She chuckled.

Barb laughed, too. "What sweet memories," she said.

"Yes, sweet memories, indeed. Then there was dad. For years, he used to dress up as Santa at the local department store. He did it as a little seasonal gig to bring in extra change to make sure my sister and I had what we needed for Christmas. After a long day of work, he would come in, throw a few logs on the fire, and make all the time in the world for us. Listening forever as we told him stories about our day... as if he didn't have a tired bone in his body. The two of them were hardworking, loving, and devoted parents. It almost seems unfair that in a blink of an eye someone could suddenly snatch them out of our lives, for good. I miss them... dearly." Her voice tapered off into a whisper.

"Oh, honey. I know it has to be especially hard during the holidays."

Clara waited a moment.

"Time has certainly helped to heal the pain. But, the close bond and the memories will never go away."

"They shouldn't. Your parents are woven into the very fabric of the beautiful woman you've become today. Beautiful inside and out," Barb said, placing her hand over Clara's.

"Thank you. I think it's important for you to know from the moment we hugged for the first time...

I knew within me I was receiving a gift in the form of a second mother. Your love and acceptance of me as your future daughter-in-law means everything to me, Barb. Not just because I'm marrying your son, but because of the empty void that I've had in my heart for so long." A tear dropped to Clara's blouse.

"Come here," Barb said.

Clara gave into her embrace, releasing the remaining tears she had left. Some tears of sadness that hadn't resurfaced in years... some were tears of joy.

"Rich and I can never replace the love of your parents, but we promise to love you in our own special way. Welcome to the family, sweetheart. Welcome to the family."

The next morning, volunteers filled the café, picking up their complimentary cup of hot chocolate before heading to their post for the day. Mackenzie invited some of her friends from Lighthouse Tours and a few of the regulars to stop by to hear her special announcement.

Mackenzie adjusted herself on a step ladder ringing a bell to gather everyone's attention.

"Good morning, friends, family, and guests of the café!" she said, wearing a Christmas hat and a cheerful smile.

She continued. "Thank you for coming out this

morning. I realize some of you are here for the hot chocolate, others for your routine breakfast, and some are here because I just sent you a text asking you to run across the street so you could be here for my exciting news." She giggled. "No matter what brought you here... thank you for taking a moment out of your day. It was about a year ago that we found ourselves in a bit of a predicament, not knowing who would take over the café once we learned it was being sold. I remember breaking out into a sweat, wondering what I was going to do, especially since I have a little girl to think about."

Folks looked at one another, some nodding in agreement and others looked concerned.

Mack noticed Brody giving her an encouraging nod from the sidelines. Clara and Mike stood a few feet behind him, absolutely clueless as to what she was about to say.

"Well, here we are again, on the brink of another change in ownership. This time because of the illness of our current owner, Mr. Garrison."

A collective sigh swept across the café as patrons listened to what Mackenzie had to say.

"My sentiments exactly. The last thing I ever wanted to hear was that Mr. Garrison was sick and not able to continue with us," she said.

A voice called out from the crowd. "Does this mean they're putting the place up for sale again? That's the last thing we need for Christmas." It was

Mrs. Dudley yelling from her booth in the corner, riling up a few of the others to a soft murmur.

"No. That's not what it means this time… not at all. Mr. Garrison offered me the opportunity to become the next owner, and… if you'll have me… then I plan to place the call later on this morning to fully accept this wonderful opportunity."

Everyone from the youngest to the eldest clapped and saluted at the idea of Mackenzie becoming the next owner. Josh was the first to give her a hearty hug, followed by each member of the team.

"Did you just say 'if we'll have you?' Are you kidding me? Of course, we'll have you. I can't think of a better fit for the position," Josh said. Josh, Dakota, Chef Harold, and Brody hovered around her, offering their congratulations.

"Mackenzie… Mackenzie… Mackenzie…" everyone chanted.

"Thank you. Wow, you sure know how to make a girl feel loved. If everyone could settle down for a moment. I just want to tell you one more thing. I promise not to take your vote of confidence lightly. I'll always serve you the same way I have over the years, whether I was a waiter, manager, or otherwise. Thank you so much for your support. I love you all," she said, blowing kisses.

Josh walked over to the jukebox. "Hey, everybody. In celebration of such a wonderful occasion, why don't we kick this morning off with a few carols?

Maybe even a group photo of the café staff so we can hang it on the wall?" he said, while popping a coin in the machine.

After the photo, Clara came over with her arms opened wide to hug her best friend.

Mack braced herself to explain. "Before you say a word, I know I didn't tell you about taking over the café, but I promise it wasn't personal," she said, squeezing her friend.

"Mack, no need to explain. With the way our schedules have been lately, I understand, and I'm so happy for you. Beyond happy. If you ask me, this is exactly what the café needed. It's what the island needed," Clara said.

"Thank you, love. Hopefully, this is only the beginning. I'd like to see Lighthouse Tours successfully take over the warehouse and send Logan back to where he belongs."

"Fingers crossed. It's completely up to the community at this point," she replied.

"Where's Jonathan and Mae? I haven't seen them this morning," Mackenzie asked.

"We're all working on a flexible schedule with family in town. They should be in later."

"Oh, that's right. I thought they may have taken off for a second honeymoon. You never know with those two lovebirds." Mack chuckled.

"I know, right? They definitely raise the bar, giving folks like us future marriage goals."

Mack and Clara joined the guys, each standing next to their man, arm in arm as they continued talking about plans for the café. Little did they know a surprise visitor from Mack's past was about to stir up the festivities.

CHAPTER 18

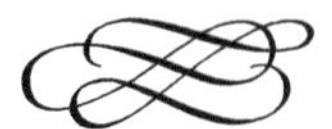

Mackenzie served the afternoon special to her regulars at the bridge table, making sure she filled their beverages to the brim. The buzz from her morning announcement had settled, but not dissipated as Josh kept the jukebox going, and folks were still asking a ton of questions about her plans as the new owner. She gladly answered and every once in a while checked the clock, waiting for Brody to return for lunch.

"One of the first things I plan to do is get one of those cute plug-in signs that light up and say open. I've always loved the way they look. It reminds me of working in an old-fashioned diner." She giggled while talking to a customer.

The bells to the front door rang and in walked a

six-foot tall, dark-bearded man who Mack recognized right away.

"Bill?" she asked, clearing her throat. She tried her best to erase the curious sound in her voice, to no avail.

"Hey, Mack." He removed his hat, nodding toward her with a generous smile across his face.

"Uhh... how are you?" she asked.

"I'm doing well. It's been a while since I stopped by to enjoy a hearty meal from the café. I thought I'd pop in and say hello."

"Ah, I see." She looked around. "Would you prefer your old spot at the front counter or —"

"Sure, that will do. I always thought this was the best seat in the house... sitting up close, near you," he said.

You've got to be kidding me, right? she thought.

"Well, go ahead and make yourself comfortable. I'm going to grab a menu for you and see if one of our servers is available to take your order. Someone should be out in just a jiffy." She desperately looked around for either Dakota or Josh, but neither of them was in sight, which was odd.

"Here you go... one menu, a placemat, and a glass of water to get you started. I'll have to go check in the back for Josh. I'm sure he just got caught up with something, not realizing another customer came in," she said, offering a brief smile.

"I'm okay with you serving me." He looked

around. "It looks like the rest of your customers are content. At least for the moment," he replied.

She glanced at the door again and then at the clock. The last thing she wanted to do was give Brody the impression that she was interested in spending time with Bill. Because she wasn't. Not even for the minimal time it would take to fulfill his order.

"It might seem that way at the moment, but we're approaching lunch hour. You know how busy it can be."

He acted as if he didn't hear her, rolling right on into his next thought. "Sooo... it's been a while. I think the last time we saw each other was at the coffee shop. What are the odds that we would both run into each other while we were on a date? So funny." He chuckled.

She didn't say much in return. Instead, she offered a closed-mouth smile.

"Mmm. Funny." She glanced around the café again, this time getting a little warm at the idea of being the only one on the floor.

"Would you hold that thought for a moment? I have to check the back and see if everything is okay."

"Sure." He smiled.

She walked away and pressed through the double doors leading to the kitchen. Immediately, she found Dakota and Josh hovering over something in the back, busying themselves to the point of not noticing her as she walked in.

Chef Harold cleared his throat to get their attention.

"What on earth are you two doing back here?" Mackenzie asked.

Josh and Dakota immediately turned around, covering up something behind them.

"Um, we're just working on a small surprise that you're not supposed to know anything about," Josh said.

Dakota chimed in. "That's right. So, if you could kindly refrain from taking another step forward, we'd appreciate it."

The tension in Mack's neck softened. She tried peering over them one more time, but it didn't work, and it was clear that Chef Harold was playing along with them.

Mack grunted.

"Okay. I won't ruin whatever it is that you're doing. However, I would appreciate a little help out front. I have an unwanted guest at the front counter and plenty of other customers that need me," she said.

"We're on it. Give us two minutes tops." Josh begged.

Mackenzie waved at him and turned around to head back to the front counter.

She flipped her dish rag over her shoulder and took out her notepad to take down Bill's order.

"Do you have any idea what you'd like to eat? We

have a couple of new popular dishes on the menu or if you're in the mood for our special, we can whip that up for you as well." She offered, getting down to it.

"Whoa, slow down a minute. I'm sure you remember how I always like to get a recommendation from you. I trust your instincts, plus you literally have the inside scoop on chef's top menu items for the day," he said.

"Bill, there really isn't much to it. All the items are delicious and cooked from scratch. It's all a matter of whether you're in the mood for fish or for --"

"You?" he replied.

"No. I was going to say fish or a corn beef sandwich." She snapped.

"Okay. I must've hit a sore spot on that one. Let me try again—"

"Bill, please don't. I'm not sure what you thought would happen by coming in here today, but I'm seeing someone. This little back and forth isn't necessary. I think it's best we just stick to your order." She added.

He placed the menu down.

"Mackenzie, I really came here to make amends. I realize now how much of a good thing I had with you and how much I messed it all up."

Her eyes widened, and her throat felt dry.

Well, isn't this something? she thought.

"There's no need to worry about making amends.

Last I recall, we had a good talk toward the end of our time dating, then we went our separate ways. You even appeared to be happy with your new friend. You know, the one that I met at the coffee shop," she replied.

"About that."

"Bill, there's really no need to explain. You're entitled to move on and live your life.

Plus, I really don't think there's a need for us to revisit the past."

"Mackenzie. Please let me talk for a moment?" he asked, looking at her with a pitiful expression.

She glanced at the clock and looked back at him, which he took as permission to proceed.

"I guess there are some lessons in life I've had to learn the hard way."

"Like, when to recognize a good woman when you have one?" she asked.

"Yes... that's certainly at the top of my list. It's just... call it poor timing, but when we were dating, I was still grappling with who I was as a man and who I wanted to become. Picture a single dad, working for close to minimum wage, hauling logs, and trying to provide for his daughter in college. Yeah, I dated every now and again, but I was a sinking ship. My main focus should've been on getting my act together. I wasn't ready to be the kind of man you needed back then."

"I see."

"Well, talk to me. Does it at least make sense to you?" he asked.

She slid her notepad into the pocket of her apron and folded her arms together.

"No, it doesn't. In all honesty, it sounds like an excuse," she replied.

"But it wasn't an excuse. I was really struggling."

"You could've been transparent about what you were going through. But you weren't. Or you could've taken a break from dating altogether, but you didn't. Instead, you moved on to someone else. So, I guess what I'm trying to say is... there were plenty of ways you could've gone about things that wouldn't have been nearly as hurtful, Bill, but you chose not to. And now, I've moved on," she said in a soft tone, determined not to be as hurtful as he had been.

"Is it the same guy you were with in the coffee shop that day? What's his name again... Brody?" he asked.

She looked toward the front window, noticing Brody exiting the doors of Lighthouse Tours, heading her way. She nodded her head toward him, signaling Bill that he was coming.

"Yes, it's the same guy. And the details of how we came to be really don't matter. The only thing that matters is that you're happy now, and you know what you want out of life. The moment you realized your shortcomings is the moment you found direction and purpose. You'll be better off for it. You and your future relationships."

Bill slouched back in his chair as if surrendering to her final words. Brody opened the front door causing the bells to jingle.

"Hey, Mack," Bill said.

"Yes?"

"I wish you all the happiness in the world. Whether it's with him or anyone else."

"Thanks." She smiled.

Just then Dakota exited from the kitchen, walking up to Bill right about the same time Brody approached the counter.

"Hi, may I take your order?" she said to Bill, giving a quick wink to Mackenzie, to relieve her of her duties.

Mackenzie leaned closer to her. "I'm not sure what you and Josh have up your sleeve, but I've got my eye on you two." Mack teased, then turned to Bill one last time, piping up so both he and Brody could hear.

"It was good seeing you, Bill. Dakota will take over from here," she said.

Brody passed Bill, sharing a friendly greeting while making his way over to Mackenzie.

"I'm sorry I'm late. I got caught up working on one of our rentals and didn't realize that time was slipping by," Brody said, kissing her on the forehead.

"It's okay, love. Josh and Dakota probably appreciated the extra time." She winked at Dakota before removing her apron and leaving with Brody for her lunch break.

~

Back at the office, Mike Sanders gazed at Dylan, the owner of the warehouse, who was sitting across from his desk. He got the general gist of what he was saying but found himself lost in his own thoughts, wondering what he would do if they didn't raise enough for the warehouse.

"Mike, what do you think?" Dylan asked.

"Huh? I'm sorry. I missed what you said. Can you repeat the question?"

"Sure, I was wondering if you had a back-up plan in mind if you guys don't raise the full twenty thousand? I still plan to give you until the first of the year as promised, but I was basically wondering if there was a contingency plan in place?" he said.

Mike slowly shook his head.

"No. Unfortunately, the fundraiser for Christmas Nights was our only plan. This hit us all so quickly, it was the best we could come up with. I'm already committed to pouring in a few dollars from Lighthouse Tours to paint the place, get it spruced up, and make sure everything is up to code. But Dylan, the initial down payment has to be generated from the locals. Not through a loan... and not through my current business. We just can't take a blow to our budget right now. I still have the North Beach location to think about."

"Understood. Trust me, from one businessman to another, I completely understand. In my heart of hearts, I'd just prefer to see you get the property over somebody like Logan Woods. He's been riding my heels just about every single week since I decided to hold off with the sale. I get the impression when the guy sees something he wants, he goes after it, fully expecting to get his way. That's the last thing we need around here. You, on the other hand, would do right by the residents and tourists of Solomons. I know you would," Dylan said.

"I appreciate the vote of confidence. Of course, the way I see it, this is all in the hands of the people of Solomons. They get to decide. Not us," Mike replied. "As we stand currently, the figures are coming in at fourteen thousand dollars, with six thousand to go. It doesn't seem like we have a lot left, but in this situation, every dollar counts, and time is winding down."

Dylan nodded along in agreement. "I'm with you, buddy. As it is, you'll need to focus on processing a new mortgage under your current business name and balance this new endeavor with everything else you have going on. It's a hefty responsibility. But, on the flip side, I think the warehouse will get a lot of traffic and will be more than capable of supplementing your income and taking care of your needs plus the needs of the island."

Mike's eyebrows furrowed together as he listened intently to everything Dylan had to say.

"And you're sure there's no way we can have an extension on the deadline? On second thought, that really wouldn't matter. By then, Christmas Nights will be over, anyway." He exhaled.

"I wish I could help you out, buddy, but my family and I plan to head further south next year. Part of our exit strategy is selling off the property we own. My wife nearly had a cow when I first told her I was taking the warehouse temporarily off the market. Once she understood what was going on, she backed down, but I can't hold out forever."

"I understand," Mike replied.

Dylan extended his hand across Mike's desk.

"Keep your head in the game. I have to believe that some way... somehow... you guys will come up with the funds. There's way too many people out here rooting for you. The odds are in your favor, Mike."

Mike shook Dylan's hand and escorted him to the front, promising that he'd be in touch soon with the final numbers.

"Thanks again for everything. Whether we're successful or not, I can't think of a more upstanding guy than you. What you did for us is honorable... giving us a chance like this... well, let's just say

Solomons will never forget your generosity." Mike smiled, giving a final hardy handshake.

Once the front door was closed, Mike rested his back against the door, making eye contact with the woman that he loved.

"How was the meeting, babe?" Clara asked.

"It was encouraging. Although, Dylan can't really do much about extending the deadline, and quite frankly, I'm not sure that an extension would help. He's at least being supportive and really rooting for us. That has to count for something, right?" he asked, sighing as he walked over to Clara's desk.

"Of course, it does. The additional support is always welcome. Even though, if this whole effort hasn't shown you just how much we're loved, then I don't know what will. Just think about it. In a very short time, we pulled the whole island together, including the local shop owners, and your parents, to do everything from volunteering, to putting on a boat parade... setting up decorations... creating a tracker for the fundraiser... you name it. This was hard work."

"You're right. And, we can't forget about Clay Nathan. The poor guy is probably going to be exhausted by the end of his vacation."

"Yeah, to think he has to hit the road and start touring again. You are loved by so many people, Mike Sanders. No matter how this turns out, don't you ever forget it," Clara said, placing a warm kiss on Mike's lips.

He chuckled. "Your kisses have a way of completely distracting me from everything I was about to say," he whispered.

"There's only one way to take care of that problem." She smiled.

"What's that?"

"We'll just have to keep kissing until you remember." Clara teased.

"I don't see how that's going to solve anything, but I'll never refuse."

"I didn't think you would," she whispered.

CHAPTER 19

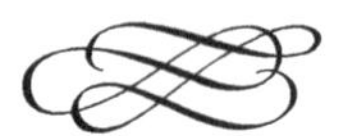

On the eve before the Christmas Nights finale, Clara Covington thundered down the stairs to the tune of holiday music and the sound of Agnes banging pots and pans. The two spent most of the day taking turns in the kitchen, preparing a last-minute menu for tonight's gathering. Having a party sounded good when the idea rolled off her tongue — but after several hours of chopping, baking, and kneading in the kitchen, she was already contemplating a nap.

Downstairs, a melodious doorbell ring chimed repeatedly— sending her dog Holly into a frenzy. She stopped behind the door drawing in the smell of her sister's pineapple upside down cake and then yelled, "How are we doing, Agnes?"

"Looking good. The hors d'oeuvres are on the

table and ready to be served and more are coming out of the oven," she replied.

"Perfect. Our guests are here."

She opened the door and was greeted by the sight of Jonathan, Mae, and their entire family, followed by Mack, Brody, and little Stephanie.

"Hi, everyone. Come on in where it's nice and warm," Clara said, revealing her smile and hugging each of them as they entered her home.

"Clara, your house looks like something right out of a Christmas card. Who did you hire to do all the decorating?" Mae asked.

She raised her hand. "Yours truly. I'll admit I had a little help from Mike and Agnes, but Joan Russell would never in a million years hire a company to decorate this place, and neither would I," she said, while continuing to take coats and jackets to hang in a nearby closet.

"Please, make yourselves comfortable. Mike will be arriving with his parents very soon. He called to say that we should go ahead and start the party without them."

Just then the doorbell rang again.

"Speaking of Mike and his parents, here they are. Go ahead and settle in. Mi casa es su casa." She chuckled.

Again, Holly lost her mind barking around the front door and pacing back and forth. The good news — the barking never lasted long. All she needed was an opportunity to sniff the guests, and then all was well in her world.

Clara opened the door.

"Hi!" She watched Mike as he entered the foyer playing with Holly. He had a fresh haircut, wore a new cardigan with slacks, and in her opinion looked effortlessly sexy.

"Hey, beautiful. Mmm, the house smells so good," he said, kissing her and then stepping aside so his parents could greet her.

Barb and Rich entered, bearing gifts.

"Clara, I really wish you would've called me over sooner. I could've helped you and Agnes prepare for this evening. The Sanders women always stick together in the kitchen. We do it to lighten the load and help keep our sanity intact." She teased.

"Well, how about we make a deal? This time you get to relax and enjoy yourself, but next time — it's on!" Clara laughed.

"You've got yourself a deal. Now where's that sweet sister of yours?" Barb said.

"Right this way."

Brody, Rich, and Mike sat with Jonathan in the living room laughing and enjoying each other's company. Steven appeared to be the ringleader of their entertainment, telling joke after joke. It made Clara feel good inside. More than anything she was happy to see Joan's home being utilized the way she had always hoped it would be.

Mack tapped Clara on the shoulder. "There you are. Stephanie and I have something for you. We figured this would be the perfect time to give you your gift," Mack said, encouraging Stephanie to present a red box with a gold ribbon.

"For me?" Clara asked.

"Actually, it's for you and Mike. Remember a little while ago, I mentioned that I had something for you?" Mack smiled.

"Yes, but you didn't have to—"

"I know, I know. But, we wanted to do something special. Technically, that gift is long overdue. It's more like an engagement slash Christmas gift, but sweet Stephanie saw it in the store, and we thought it was absolutely perfect. Isn't that right, sweetheart?" Mack asked, brushing Stephanie's hair back.

Stephanie nodded.

"Mommy and I liked it so much that we had to buy it for you and Mr. Mike. But you can't open it until Christmas morning. No peeking, okay?"

Clara laughed. "Okay, I promise. I'll tell you what. How about you go find the perfect spot under the tree for me? That way I won't be tempted to try and guess what it is."

"Okay." Stephanie skipped off leaving the two women to talk.

Mack waited a moment then leaned in and whispered, "So, how's it going with the in-laws? You look as if you're all getting along really well."

"Mack, I don't know how I got to be so lucky. All the anxiety I had about meeting them for the first time has completely washed away. Rich is amazing, and Barb... she's comforting... easy to talk to. I think we're all going to make a great team."

"Aww, I'm so glad to hear it. The Sanders family... Clara Sanders... it sounds like music to my ears. Now, all you have to do is set a date."

"I know. It's been quite the talk lately. I honestly could get married at any time. I'd marry Mike tomorrow if he were willing. All that matters is that I have him in my life," Clara said, glancing over his way.

"Oh, I'll bet."

"You know, Mack. It just dawned on me... everything Joan ever wished for me has come true. I can look around this room and see evidence of it all around us. I finally have love in my life, my family, and I'm filling this place with joy and laughter... it's exactly what she wanted," Clara said.

"You see there. All you had to do was trust and believe everything would work out... plus have a little patience."

"Yeah," Clara responded in a dreamy voice.

The sound of a utensil tapping on glass interrupted their conversation.

"Good evening, everyone. As Clara's sister and chef for tonight, I'd like to officially announce there are hot hors d'oeuvres and delectable desserts waiting for you in the dining area. Please... eat and be merry!" Agnes said, melodiously.

Clara raised her finger to inject one additional thought.

"Thanks, sis, for your culinary skills. God knows I couldn't have made it through the day without the extra help. As for everyone else, you are all family to us. I know you're ready to dig in and I won't stand in your way. Mike and I just wanted to thank you again from the bottom of our hearts for everything you've done for Christmas Nights." She motioned toward him to come and say a few words.

"Yes, and no matter what the outcome may be tomorrow, I feel good in my heart that we've given this our all. Should Logan Woods establish his company here in Solomons, then we will still work day and night giving the best island tours and rental experience possible... even until the very end," he said, ending on a somber note.

"There will be no end." Mae professed.

"We hope not, but we all should be prepared for whatever comes our way. If his business should move in and drive more traffic than ours, then we have to be ready to face the music." Mike offered.

"Let's keep it positive, Mike. It ain't over yet," Brody said.

Jonathan piped up while refilling his glass. "Hey, Mike, where are we with the numbers? Are we getting close to our goal?"

"Close but no cigars. As of late this afternoon, the count was at fourteen thousand, five hundred dollars. But, like Brody said, we're going to keep it positive and hope for the best. Like Clara said earlier... a huge thank you. We truly appreciate all that you've done. Now as Agnes said, let's all eat and be merry." Mike cheered.

On Christmas Eve, the chime from the clock near the gazebo vibrated throughout the area, striking six. It was a brisk evening, with a constant breeze from the nearby water and a perfect moon that shone brightly over the dock. Children lined up to stuff last minute letters to Santa in a nearby box, and Clay Nathan stood on the side of the stage, positioning himself to sing one last song for the grand finale of Christmas Nights.

Mayor Thompson took the stage.

"Good evening, ladies and gentlemen."

Jonathan, Mae, and her family, their neighbor Meredith, Mike, Clara, Agnes, and all the staff of Lighthouse Tours gathered with the crowd.

"Well... here we are... I can't believe it's already the last night that we're gathering. I can clearly remember when the truck rolled in, filled with decorations to line the streets of Solomons Island, and now it's Christmas Eve. Before I announce our grand total to you, thank you to every person who helped to make this event possible. From those that decorated, to the volunteers, and our very own Clay Nathan."

The crowd cheered. Clara looked around, noticing significantly more people than she'd seen in weeks past, and was hoping it would make a difference.

Mayor Thompson, please tell us something good, she thought.

Mike tugged her toward his side, wrapping his arm around her shoulders.

"Without further ado, it's time to announce the total amount of funds raised from Christmas Nights so far."

Jan unveiled the chart, revealing a thermometer that displayed how much was raised.

"To the residents and guests of Solomons Island, because of your generosity, we are currently at fifteen thousand dollars," Mayor Thompson said.

A somber tone fell over the crowd.

"Now, I realize at first glance, it may disappoint some of you because we haven't reached our goal yet. But, I personally cannot take this number lightly. We may be a small island, but clearly there's lots of love going around this place in order to raise this much in such a short period of time. Besides the fifteen thousand, so many business owners have been reporting record sales... greater than any year prior. I don't know about you, but I think that's worth celebrating." He continued.

Mike and Clara looked at each other while Rich and Barb offered words of encouragement for a job well done. Several feet behind Mike, Clara caught a glimpse of Logan Woods with a smirk on his face. It nearly made her feel ill, but she shifted her attention to the stage.

"Sylvester is right, you know," she said.

"I know. But, somehow, it still doesn't stop this feeling of disappointment inside," Mike replied.

"Excuse me —" a woman's voice yelled from the back of the crowd.

"Excuse me, Mayor Thompson. Over here—" She waved.

The mayor squinted as he looked out into the crowd.

"Yes, ma'am. Can I help you?" he said.

The hunched over lady stepped forward.

"I'd like to donate a check to match the money we've already raised. The money is on behalf of myself and the bridge club of Solomons. Ladies, please step forward," Ms. Violet said, waving to the members.

She continued. "Mike Sanders and his employees have been showcasing this beautiful island and its surrounding attractions for years. My club can't think of a better, more deserving person to run the new warehouse than Mike and everyone at Lighthouse Tours." She bumped into Logan Woods, knocking him aside so she could get closer to the front stage. As each lady passed, Logan received another bump, causing him to step even further out of the way.

The mayor stood in disbelief. "Let me get this straight. Your club is donating fifteen thousand dollars?" he asked.

"That's right. We had a little spare change set aside among the members and thought this was a worthy cause to donate to. Now... hopefully, all the money combined will more than help cover the down payment." She hesitated. "And help send that turkey standing in the crowd back to where he belongs," she said, directing her attention toward Logan.

Woods took one last look around him and marched away with a grim expression on his face.

The mayor continued. "It's rare that I'm at a loss for words... Mike... Clara... would you guys like to come up and say something to the crowd?" He smiled and then shook the ladies' hands before stepping to the side.

Mike skipped a few steps, quickly making his way up, with Clara following closely behind.

"Ladies, I could hug each and every one of you."

"We don't mind if you do." Ms. Violet teased.

He smiled.

"You deserve so much more, but for now I want

to say a huge thank you on behalf of Lighthouse Tours and our entire Solomons family. This is truly a Christmas miracle... one that will provide so many with permanent housing for their boats, and one that just may have helped save Lighthouse Tours in the long run."

He turned to Clara. "Do you have anything to add?"

But before she could respond, Mackenzie shouted from the crowd, "Free meals and hot chocolate for the bridge club of Solomons Island!" And the crowd went absolutely wild with cheers and hugs in celebration and support of Lighthouse Tours. It was the perfect cue for Clara and Mike to hug the ladies and then clear the stage to make way for Clay Nathan and his rendition of Silent Night.

As he sang, young children ran playfully around their parents' legs, lovers stood with their arms locked together, and Clara and Mike, Jonathan and Mae, and Brody and Mackenzie, shared a congratulatory embrace with their significant other. It was one of the greatest nights the island had experienced in a very long time.

Are you ready to continue on to book five? Continue reading!

ALSO BY MICHELE GILCREST

Beachfront Memories: Solomons Island Book Five

She's forty-two, with a broken past, and currently on a sabbatical from dating.

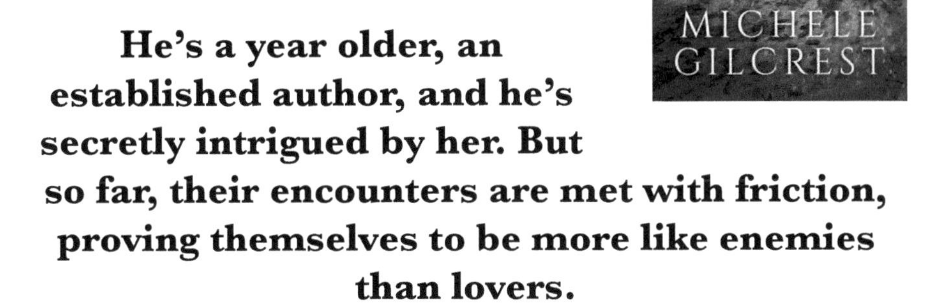

He's a year older, an established author, and he's secretly intrigued by her. But so far, their encounters are met with friction, proving themselves to be more like enemies than lovers.

Will his wit and charm win her over? Or will her strong will and determination draw a permanent line of division between them?

Agnes Covington is a waitress by day and has high aspirations of starting her own food truck business. Who has time for men? At least that's what she thinks. Besides, with her proven track record of failed relationships, she's doubtful this would be any different.

Grant is renting a beach house on the island while writing his next novel. His three-month stay is supposed to be temporary, yet inspirational as he surrounds himself among the scenic views. But will a spark of love keep him on the island a little longer than expected?

Neither of them is looking for love, plus they're always at odds. But, once she observes his tenderness, will it win Agnes over, causing her to break her sabbatical?

If you enjoy clean, romantic beach reads, featuring love over forty, grab your copy today!